The VOYAGE of LUCY P. SIMMONS
LUCY AT SEA

The VOYAGE of LUCY P. SIMMONS
LUCY AT SEA

BARBARA MARICONDA

KATHERINE TEGEN BOOKS
An Imprint of HarperCollins Publishers

Katherine Tegen Books is an imprint of HarperCollins Publishers.

The Voyage of Lucy P. Simmons: Lucy at Sea
Copyright © 2013 by Barbara Mariconda
For information address HarperCollins Children's Books,
a division of HarperCollins Publishers, 10 East 53rd Street,
New York, NY 10022.
www.harpercollinschildrens.com

Library of Congress Cataloging-in-Publication Data
Mariconda, Barbara.
  Lucy at sea / Barbara Mariconda. – First edition.
    pages cm. – (The voyage of Lucy P. Simmons)
  Summary: "Lucy travels to Australia in her magical house-turned-ship
to find her long-lost Aunt Pru and solve the mystery of the curse on her
family"– Provided by publisher.
  ISBN 978-0-06-211993-3 (hardcover bdg.)
  [1. Orphans–Fiction. 2. Dwellings–Fiction. 3. Magic–Fiction.
4. Household employees–Fiction. 5. Aunts–Fiction. 6. Blessing and
cursing–Fiction. 7. Australia–History–20th century–Fiction. 8. Sea
stories.] I. Title.
PZ7.M33835Luc 2013   2012051735
[Fic]–dc23   CIP
                                                                AC

Typography by Amy Ryan
13 14 15 16 17 CG/RRDH 10 9 8 7 6 5 4 3 2 1
❖
First Edition

To Annie Dichele and Alphonse DeJulio—
for being the wind in my sails,
be the seas calm or stormy

1

August 26, 1906

The ship's bell clanged riotously as we dropped anchor in the Port of Boston.

Marni, Walter, Addie, and I had maneuvered the *Lucy P. Simmons* respectably past Winthrop Peninsula, around Deer Island, between a three-masted, wooden-hulled barge and more two-masted brigs than I could count, all the while flanked by fishing schooners, a deep-water cargo carrier, and even a steam-powered tug. Father would have been proud!

Of course, I wondered, how much of this

seamanship was actually the result of our sailing skills? After all, the *Lucy P. Simmons* was no ordinary ship! And ours, no ordinary voyage.

"Play us a tune, Lucy!" Annie shouted. "To celebrate!" She looked from me to her brother Georgie, her blond hair whipped by the wind, blue eyes sparkling.

"Yes—the one where we join in on the ending," Georgie urged.

From the pocket of my overalls I pulled the flute of whalebone and hardwood that Father had carved during his days at sea. As the hull of our schooner creaked and moaned against the pilings, I put the instrument to my lips. Gazing at the hustle and bustle on the pier, accompanied by the cries of raucous gulls, my fingers flew over the tone holes, improvising a lilting melody. As always, I finished with that mysterious tune Father had taught me, the one so old the words had been forgotten, except for a snippet of refrain: *A la dee dah dah . . . a la dee dah dee. . . .* My makeshift little family hummed along on the wordless verses, then, as always, sang out on the *la dee dah dee*s. Pugsley ran in circles around us, his small curly tail wagging wildly, howling along with each high note.

"Enough!" Marni ordered. "No time for dawdling! We need to dry her jibs, swab down the deck, hire a crew, and buy provisions enough for a lengthy voyage." Marni's long silver hair hung along her back in a single braid, and her weathered face gave her the look of a dignified, wise Indian brave.

Addie patted my shoulder reassuringly. "'Tis a lovely tune, Miss Lucy, I'll give ye that! But Marni's right. There's much to be done if we're goin' to sail away and find your auntie Pru. Australia's a long way off, it 'tis! We'd better be gettin' on with it, lass." Aunt Pru! Addie was right—there wasn't a moment to lose!

Annie and Georgie's older brother, Walter, was already lowering the gangplank, providing a bridge from deck to dock. After the strange and spectacular events back at Simmons Point, and our resulting overnight sail down to Boston, it would be good to feel solid ground beneath my feet. And to get a bite to eat. My stomach rumbled and groaned. What with the extraordinary events that took place, it was hard to recall when we'd had our last full meal. "What about Pugsley?" I asked.

"Best t' leave 'im 'ere, where he won't go and get himself lost," Addie replied. "Ye'd all be broken-hearted without the wee pup, ye would."

With a flimsy length of rope, I tied him to a brass cleat on deck. "Stay, Pugsley!" I commanded. Annie pointed a finger. "STAY!" she repeated. Though he shimmied and whined as we marched across the gangplank, I was unworried. The dog had an uncanny sense of being in the right place at the right time.

The six of us headed along the pier and cobbled streets lined with rows of brick warehouses, pubs, and shops. The whole of the waterfront was abuzz with activity—draymen drove mules hauling flat wagons piled with wood and bricks, rough-and-tumble sailors in sturdy work pants topped with billowy shirts and neckerchiefs moved barrels of pungent salt cod and salmon. Seamen pushed provision carts loaded down with canvas-covered parcels of every size. Others flowed in and out of the grog and ale shops, their tongues and joints loosened from the spirits served. Here a pile of granite blocks from the Maine quarries, there a cargo of grain from the Midwest. Farther along we passed a coal schooner tied up beside a sleek Hawaiian vessel loaded with sugarcane, gazed up at the tall spars that drove it across the wild oceans. Cattle lowed from the hold of another ship, while salesmen onshore hawked their wares and services: "Yachts to let by the hour, day, or season! Competent skippers furnished as desired! Come to Robert Bibber's Beach House!"

"Stay together!" Marni commanded, grabbing Annie's hand and tugging Georgie, who had stopped to gape at the crisscross webs of rigging and the spearlike bowsprits aiming toward shore from the prows of many ships. I noticed a group of old, ruddy-faced men crouched in a circle mending nets, singing another song of the sea that Father had taught me:

> *"The ship it was their coffin and their grave it*
> *was the sea!*
> *A-sailing down all on the coasts of High Barbaree."*

I joined my voice in their song, until Marni gently muffled my lips with her hand. The old salts smiled toothless grins as she chastised me. "The likes of them are not your mates," she whispered. "Best not to stir their attention!" Addie reiterated the sentiment, her fingers pressed against the small of my back, bringing up the rear with Walter. A group of younger sailors whistled as we passed, shamelessly ogling Addie's delicate features, golden-brown hair swept into a twist, small waist, and prim carriage. She blushed and trained her hazel eyes steadfastly in the opposite direction, pretending not to notice them.

"Fisher and Fairbanks Rock Cordials for coughs and lung troubles! Buy a tin here!" The man wore a pair of wooden signs that hung around his neck, sandwiching him front and back.

A boy about Georgie's age, in patched trousers

and shirt, a cap pulled jauntily atop his bowl-cut hair, waved a newspaper from a large linen sack. "Get your paper here! Read all about it! Freak hurricane destroys Maine mansion! Sightings of a specter ship? Or the ramblings of a madman? You decide! Get yer paper here!"

I stopped short, heart pounding. Addie walked up my heel and bumped against me. "Good lord, child, what is it?" I pointed toward the newsboy and groped in my pocket for a coin, but Walter had already pressed a nickel into the lad's hand.

"Walter, read it! What does it say?"

He folded the paper and tucked it under his arm. "Not here . . . too many curious eyes and ears."

"Hardy food and grog!" a busty woman shouted from a tavern doorway. "Hot soup and biscuits!"

"In there," Marni said, raising her chin in the direction of the threshold. "But wait." She quickly hid her braid inside the collar of her work shirt. Walter removed the cap from his dark straight hair and handed it to me. "Let's try to pass you off as a boy," he whispered. "That head of red curls will draw attention we don't want!" I took the cap and shoved my wild tresses up underneath. One . . . two . . . three . . . four attempts before the last of the stubborn auburn locks were concealed.

We headed inside to a table along the back wall. It was a loud, rough-and-tumble establishment, with tables full of mariners and crewmen eating their fill. Some argued good-naturedly, others shouted for second helpings. They ate with much gusto, swabbing their plates with biscuits and rashers of bacon, wiping their whiskered mouths on their sleeves. Others slurped soup and guzzled what was left, lifting bowls to mouths with dirty hands.

"What'll it be fer ye?" a woman called. She sidled up to the table, licked the stub of a pencil. "Breakfast fare or soup and biscuits? Ale or coffee? Hard cider?"

Marni nodded to Walter. "Breakfast for all," he said. "Eggs, bacon. Hotcakes. Coffee. Milk for the little ones here, if you will, ma'am."

"Done," she proclaimed, scribbling on her order pad. And she was gone.

"Let's see what they're saying," Marni murmured. Walter nodded, spread the paper out on the table, and began to read in a soft, measured voice. We all leaned toward him. I stared at the columns of newsprint as he read:

"Portland, Maine August 25, 1906
Freak Storm Destroys Maine Mansion
North of Portland, in a secluded area of mid-coast Maine known locally as Simmons Point, a freak hurricane was reported to have rolled in suddenly, devastating the home of the late

Captain Edward Simmons. The storm was unusual in that it apparently only touched shore at Simmons Point, bringing wind and waves so violent as to overtake the shorefront mansion and catapult it into the raging sea. Curiously, the only victim found was that of a local judge, the Honorable Albert Forester, whose lifeless body washed ashore at a nearby beach. The remains of the other inhabitants of the home—the heir apparent, twelve-year-old Lucille P. Simmons, and her legal guardians, Victor and Margaret Simmons, as well as the longtime Simmons family caretaker, Miss Addie Clancy—have not been found."

Annie clamped a hand over her mouth. Walter glanced up at us. "Go on," I urged. He cleared his throat and continued:

"In recent years, the Simmons family had been plagued with a curse of tragic events. Lucille's parents, Captain Edward and his wife, Johanna, were drowned in a boating accident last spring. Accompanied by daughter Lucille, they reportedly set out for an afternoon sail when a squall rolled in. It is believed that the Simmonses, in an attempt to rescue a man

in a disabled vessel, capsized, resulting in the drownings of the captain and his missus. Young Lucille was saved by an unknown hero, her near lifeless body dragged to shore."

My eyes met Marni's and she nodded ever so slightly.

"Court records indicate that in Simmons's last will and testament, an aunt, Prudence Simmons, was named overseer of the estate and guardian of young Lucille. Unable to locate Miss Prudence, who is said to be a world traveler and adventuress, the court appointed the next of kin, the captain's brother, Victor, and his wife, Margaret, to care for the child and the property. They were in residence at the time of the aforementioned storm. Questions about a reported family fortune abound, evidence of which must have been swept to sea with the house."

Walter paused, collected himself, and went on:

"The only eyewitness to this most recent tragic spectacle, one Jeremiah Perkins, was said to have been overcome with hysteria, spouting

the ravings of a madman, and we quote:

"'They were in there, in the mansion, the whole sorry bunch, with the Seahag leading the way! She's a siren, I tell you, a witch of the sea, with that long silver hair and sea-glass green eyes! Stole my kids, Walter and Georgie, the baby Annie, and even my good-for-nothin' dog! She caused it, I tell you, the swirling up of the wind and churning of waves like no human's seen before! I followed the lot of them into the mansion, got caught in the assault of the sea. The ocean swell crashed in, filled the hallways, and rocked her off her foundation!'

"Perkins, it is said, paused, sweating profusely, wiping his brow with a dirty rag. He continued:

"'I tell you, the entire house, she flipped upside down and into the deep!' Here Perkins began to shake uncontrollably. His lips trembled in an attempt to speak. 'And, amidst a great creaking and moaning, the house changed, floor to rafter, and I swear to the Almighty creator, each timber and shingle transformed into parts of a sailing ship! Windows became portholes, curtains whipped into sails. I tell you, the house sailed away, she did, in a swirl of supernatural glittering mist. A specter ship, with the siren,

the uppity little red-headed miss and her Irish nanny, my youngins and pug dog aboard.'

"*The editor adds, after some investigative inquiry, that Perkins, known for his affinity for spirits, is likely not a reliable witness. However, it is interesting to note that not a scrap of the Simmonses' mansion or any victims of the said event have washed ashore, aside from the judge. Rumors of a family curse persist. Locals, captured by the intrigue of this tale, have their eyes peeled to the horizon. Specter ship, or the ramblings of a madman? You decide!*"

Alongside the news story were two engravings—the first, an artist's rendering of the pile of rubble in the gaping space overlooking the shore at Simmons Point, where my beautiful home once stood. Beside it, a remarkably accurate sketch of my own face stared back at me—based, I could see, on my school portrait, taken before the accident. I looked like a different person then, and I was. For a moment my heart ached for all I'd lost, for the life with Mother and Father I used to have. But after many months' time, I realized that allowing grief to overpower me wasn't going to help. It would take every ounce of energy and determination to find Aunt Pru—my only living relative. And it was only

Pru who could help me unlock the mystery of the curse that had already taken the lives of my mother and father—and nearly mine as well.

We looked around, one to the other. My fingers flew to my cap, checking for any tell-tale tendrils that might give us away. I wondered, too, how my friends felt having their father described as a madman. I could almost feel Walter's anger, Georgie's shame, Annie's fear. "They can say what they will about your pa," Marni said, as if reading my thoughts, "but never was there a more accurate account—except, of course, for the part about the Seahag!" She smiled with her pale green eyes and patted Annie's and my hands. "But now that the facts are out there, there's little time to waste. Men of the sea are a superstitious lot. We'll need to procure what we need and set sail before they put two and two together."

Walter folded the paper as the tavern maid approached with our tray of steaming fare. Our plates were passed, and in keeping with the apparent custom in this establishment, we manhandled our forks in fisted hands and ate ravenously. In this place a napkin in the lap, an extended pinkie from the handle of a coffee mug would surely arouse attention. As we shoveled our food into our mouths a group of old-timers sat, just a table away, their scrubby-whiskered faces inclined toward the newspaper one of them held open wide. His large, knobby hands shook the newsprint pages with a flourish. Scraps of his dramatic reading cut through the din in the restaurant: *assault of the sea . . . specter ship . . . Seahag . . . rumors of a curse . . . siren . . .* and my family name, repeated many times . . . *Simmons . . . Simmons. . . .*

A curious crowd began to form about the reader, not ten feet from where we sat. I could feel their excitement billow and whip around them like the sails of a ship, filling and expanding, gathering energy around the tale.

Annie and Georgie shrank in their seats. Addie sank back in her chair. Marni, elbow propped on the table, tipped her forehead against her palm. A wave of worry crashed over me. If the authorities discovered we were here in Boston, no doubt we'd be detained. Questioned. And how could we possibly explain the miraculous events that had transpired? Worse, would we be accused of some wrong-doing? Of murdering the judge? Walter pressed a few coins into the tavern maid's hand to cover our meal along with a modest gratuity, and with due haste we set about making our final plans.

I looked between Marni and Addie and the Perkins clan. We would need to purchase what we needed with speed and stealth. We could not set sail soon enough.

2

While still at table, Marni had created a quick inventory of supplies to ready our ship for an extended voyage. How she knew what we'd need was a mystery, as was just about everything about her. My eyes traveled down her scrawled list:

manila rope	belaying pins
oil	brooms
wire seizing	sail needles
arsenic	brass screws
shovels	lanyards
caulking frow	carpenter's tools
tarpaulin	duck sailcloth
deck lighter	

By the time I took it all in, my heart was pounding. Caulking frow? Arsenic? Belaying pins? Despite the fact that I was a sea captain's daughter, I had little working knowledge of day-to-day life aboard ship, of the necessary maintenance to keep a vessel seaworthy. The scope of our endeavor suddenly struck me. I was ill prepared for such a task, and ignorant of all but the most rudimentary skills. I glanced at Walter, who met my eyes and quickly looked away. Addie bit her bottom lip. "I might be speakin' out o' place," she said, her Irish brogue thicker than usual, "and perhaps I'm the only one worryin'. But do ye think we're up t' this? Australia's a world away."

Eyes fixed on the list, Marni spoke. "We'll be hiring an experienced crew. And I grew up aboard ships, amidst seafaring. Lucy has it in her blood. And Walter possesses the benefit of youth, strength, and courage, plus the leadership he's shown in the care of his siblings." She looked up, caught my eye. "And I do believe the *Lucy P. Simmons* will not let us down. We know she's equipped with—how shall I say it—extraordinary qualities."

"What about me?" Georgie piped in. "I'll be a big help!" Then, a shadow of worry creased his brow. "But what about food? We'll need to eat to stay strong!"

"Georgie, I'll make you first mate," Marni

replied, "right after we purchase our food stores and set sail." She began penciling a second list:

one hundredweight of beef
five barrels of pork
five barrels of flour
five barrels of hardtack
three barrels of herring
two barrels of cider

This was no regular grocery list. It would clearly be a long, difficult passage.

"All right," Marni said, folding the paper, slipping the pencil behind her ear. "Let's get to it! Not a moment to lose!" We left the table in quiet groups of two, so as not to attract notice. Marni and Annie, followed by Addie and Georgie, then Walter and me, all walking along the perimeter of the room, in different directions, toward the door.

It felt good to breathe the sharp, salty air outside, but I was suddenly conscious of curious eyes all around us—or perhaps it was my imagination. We continued to walk in inconspicuous pairs until Marni found what she was looking for. The sign in front of the large wooden structure read: BRADFORD AND EAST DRY DOCK COMPANY AND CHANDLERY GOODS. She nodded to Walter, and the two of them went inside, one at a time. Addie and Annie strolled, hand in hand, along the waterfront, leaving Georgie and me to while away a bit of time.

A good ways down the pier, a square-rigger was docked, its crewmen scurrying like monkeys, working the lines. "Look!" Georgie shouted, running ahead. "Come on, let's watch!"

I walked slowly behind him, my eyes traveling up along the maze of masts and yards, booms, and gaffs. The sail was set "square to"—perpendicular to the length of the ship. I watched a man scramble up to a semicircular platform set at a lower masthead, where he proceeded to tinker with the rigging. Father had shown me pictures of such ships, which I'd looked at with great interest. But great interest does not translate into working knowledge. The hardy breakfast I'd so eagerly devoured lay heavily in my gut, and the excitement and anticipation I'd felt when we miraculously set sail seeped out of me like sour milk.

A hand clasped my shoulder. "What's the matter, lad?" a voice demanded. "Yearnin' fer a life at sea, are ye?"

I spun around in the direction of the voice belonging to a scrappy-looking sailor, his face sliced diagonally with a long purplish scar from eyebrow to opposite cheek. A dirty red bandana was pulled tightly around his forehead, tied in back. A fringe of greasy, straggly hair hung beneath it. His fingers pressed painfully into the hollow between my neck and shoulder. I recoiled, but he grabbed my wrist and held tight.

"Georgie!" I yelled, squirming, trying to free myself from his grip.

"No need to call for your little friend—lookie there—my mate's already bringing 'im on board for a better view." He laughed—a dry raspy cackle—and yanked me forward. To my horror, sure enough, there was Georgie, another brute dragging him, kicking and hollering, his cries lost in the commotion of the waterfront.

I tried to scream, but no sound emerged. I threw myself down on the pier, a heap of dead weight, kicking and thrashing with all my might until my voice found its way to my lips. "Somebody! Help! Help!"

"I didn't think ye had it in ye," the man said, clamping a filthy hand over my mouth and jerking me to my feet. "Yep, a cabin boy needs a bit o' spit 'n' vinegar to survive at sea!" His palm tasted of metal and salt. I bit down, hard, and felt the flesh give way. I spat blood. He cursed and threw me back to the ground, wrenched my arm violently behind my back. "That'll be the last time ye try that trick!" he snarled. My face pressed against the ground. I inhaled dirt and sand. Still I kicked and struggled. Suddenly there was a flurry of yipping and growling, a commotion of small paws raising up a cloud of dust.

"Pugsley!" I shouted. My loyal companion grabbed hold of the man's ragged pants and tugged furiously.

"What on *earth*? Unhand that boy, I tell you!"

A pair of polished black boots stopped inches from my face. My eyes crossed as I forced them into focus.

"Georgie! The other one's got Georgie!" I yelled, flailing with my one available arm, grit and gravel biting into my lips and cheek. My fingers crawled to the pointed toe of the gentleman's boot, and grabbed hold of his ankle for dear life. Pugsley continued ripping, tearing, and growling in a fearsome tug-of-war with my captor's grimy trousers.

"I say," boomed the distinguished voice, "release both lads or I'll hand you over to the authorities! I'm wise to your game, pressing unfortunates into your service. Unhand him! Now!"

"Have it your way," my tormentor replied. "I have no use for the likes of 'im—'twas one of those delinquents hangin' about. Beggin' for a chance at sea, he was, then after I oblige him the opportunity, he changes his mind. Go on—go!" He shoved me away, and finally shook Pugsley from his leg. I stumbled to my feet, turning wildly in the direction of the square-rigged ship. "Georgie! Where's—"

"Released, as well—see—here he comes now." The gentleman sailor, in the finely cut navy jacket and black leather boots, nodded over his shoulder.

Georgie, wiping his mouth with the back of his hand, swaggered toward us. Pugsley leaped in joyful circles at his feet.

"Did you see me fight him off?" Georgie shouted. "Did you see, Lucy?"

I cringed. Georgie gasped and sputtered, our savior looking curiously between us. "I meant Lou . . . Louie!" Georgie corrected pathetically, drawing even more attention. My hand flew to my cap, captured a long curl, and shoved it quickly back under the brim.

The gentleman raised an eyebrow.

"Thank you, sir," I said, in the deepest-pitched voice I could muster. "We must be going. We are eternally in your debt." I grabbed Georgie by the shirt sleeve and pulled him along as hastily as I could.

"Are you—*boys*—alone here?"

I winced at his inflection on the word *boys*. "Oh, not to worry," I called over my shoulder, my voice cracking. "We're meeting our party shortly. Thank you again!"

My rubbery knees carried us back toward the dry goods store. Pugsley trotted beside us, tongue lolling. I dared not look back.

"I'm sorry, Lucy, I didn't mean—"

"Stop *calling* me that! People will hear you!"

"I know, it's just—"

"Sh! We'll be in trouble enough—we almost got kidnapped, do you realize that?"

"Nah, I fought him off. . . ."

I rolled my eyes. "It was that gentleman who stepped in—if not for him . . ."

Tears sprang to my eyes as the implications of what might have happened hit me. I could hardly believe I'd nearly forfeited my quest to find Aunt Pru before it had really begun. My thoughts suddenly turned to Mother and Father—their high hopes, their confidence in my ability to make them proud. And the very idea of letting Marni down, or Addie, was nearly as distressing as disappointing Mother and Father. I cringed. "Not a word of this to Marni," I whispered. "Or Addie. Not a scrap of it to anyone, do you hear? They don't need to worry about this."

"Oh, but I want to tell Walter about the brawl, how we—"

"Not a word!" I snapped, tightening my grip on his arm. "Promise! Swear on your mother's grave!"

His eyes rounded like saucers and I felt a jab of regret at my unfortunate choice of words. But I steeled myself and squeezed all the harder.

"But . . ." he stammered.

"Swear it!" I hissed.

Georgie pouted and shrugged. I twisted his arm. "Swear!"

"All right! All right! I swear." He threw me a black look.

"Good!" I shot a glance over my shoulder to make certain we weren't being followed. "There's Marni and Walter."

They'd emerged from the Bradford and East Drydock Company, trailed by several clerks laden with supplies. Walter whistled sharply for a provision cart, and an old man with a sway-backed donkey wheeled about. We watched as they piled on the many crates and barrels that would be our sustenance at sea. Marni peered across the dock and caught my eye, and motioned for us to follow. There, off to the side, were Addie and Annie. We all proceeded at discrete distances, again, so as not to arouse suspicion, especially since the newsboy still paced back and forth, hawking his papers along the waterfront.

Finally, the hull of the *Lucy P. Simmons* appeared. I couldn't wait to get aboard, away from prying eyes and unscrupulous interests of all kinds. Once the provisions were loaded under Marni's watchful eye, and after Addie and Annie climbed aboard, I grabbed Georgie and made a run for it across the gangplank, Pugsley at our heels.

As our feet crossed from solid ground to the safety of my ship, I heaved a sigh of relief and chanced one last glance over my shoulder.

There, to my dismay, a few hundred yards off, stood the gentleman sailor in his navy jacket and shiny black boots. He stared intently at our ship over the top of the newspaper he held open in his outstretched arms.

3

As Marni, Walter, and Georgie stowed the supplies, a heaviness descended upon me. Addie had gone off with Annie to read a story, and Pugsley snored through his pushed-in snout in a sunny corner of the deck in a coil of rope beside the mainmast.

I walked around the ship, running my hand along her smooth timbers, recalling what she'd been before her strange metamorphosis. Looking at the cabin wall, it was easy to recognize the handsome wainscoting that had once trimmed our dining room back in Maine. As I descended the steps to the lower deck, my hand encircled the polished curve of handrail that had previously graced the sweeping staircase in our center hall. I was, at once, filled with longing for what used to be, and at the same time grateful for vestiges of the past that had miraculously become part of the present.

I wandered about curiously, as none of us had thoroughly explored, shocked and overwhelmed as we were at the events that had set us afloat in the first place.

Oh, what a beautiful, unusual vessel it was! I could almost feel Father's presence, his pride in the fine workmanship and delight in the elegant details of design. I pressed my forehead to a brass-trimmed porthole, catching a glimpse of the figurehead that still caused my heart to rattle in my chest. Aunt Margaret and Uncle Victor—or what was left of them—wooden outstretched arms reaching for far horizons, their terrified expressions eternally captured, looking out to sea. I turned from them—after all, they'd gotten what they'd wanted, hadn't they? To be permanent fixtures in the Simmons estate . . . though not exactly in the way they'd imagined.

My feet carried me toward an ornately carved oak door. I twisted the crystal knob and slipped inside. It took my eyes a moment to adjust to the dim light. When the room came into focus I gasped.

It was the chart room—so like Father's library at home that I was nearly overcome with nostalgia. On the far wall hung the painting of Ulysses and his capsized ship, the silver-haired siren beckoning him from the churning ocean. Here, the shelves of books, there his desk and chair, and, in the corner, the set of long flat drawers holding charts of the many routes Father had traveled during his years at sea. I hastened toward the map chest, hoping it contained valuable information we'd need to set our course to Australia. But a blue-backed chart spread out atop the desk caught my eye. Its curled edges were held down by four heavy, glass orbs, one in each corner.

I leaned over the chart, marked with dotted lines and dates to indicate the course and time-line of a voyage, the land and oceans spread out flat. There it was—Australia! My heart raced. Some-where on that continent was my aunt Pru! My finger traced the line from the Atlantic coast out toward the Azores, sweeping down along the western coast of Africa, around the Cape of Good Hope and the Indian Ocean, and on to Australia! As if Father had laid it out for us himself!

Encouraged, I turned, and something else caught my eye—a large rectangular chest crafted of steel and brass nestled in a narrow alcove. I had a vague recollection of seeing this somewhere in the house—yes—it had been stowed in the back of the closet in the study. Father's safe! I knelt before it, reaching with trembling fingers for the circular knob, its circumference engraved with small white numbers. Around the mechanism was a collection of scratches and dents—surely evidence of Uncle Victor's miserable attempts to get at whatever was inside. For what precious secrets it might hold! The round ridged dial was cool to the touch. I spun it to the right, then left, and right again, listening for a secret click, but, of course, there was none. The exact series of numbers that could unbolt the sturdy strong box would be impossible to guess.

The combination must be somewhere. I turned back to the desk, sat in Father's chair, and pulled open one drawer after another, rifling through them. A fountain pen, a pair of cuff links, a small tin of tacks, a whittled-down pencil, a collection of stationery embossed with Mother's initials: *JS*. These simple objects that had passed so casually through my parents' hands filled my eyes with tears. I brought each item to my face, so that I could intimately touch what they'd touched. Traced my finger along the initials on Mother's note cards. I sniffed, ran them along my cheek, all in a futile attempt to capture some essence of what was lost.

Enough! To shake off the melancholy that threatened to overtake me, I abruptly stood, hands on hips, and directed my attention back to the imposing metal safe, anxious to discover whatever it might hold. Family secrets. Information about my aunt. Some clue about the curse. Or resources. The satchel of money we'd brought from Maine wouldn't last forever—a good portion was already spent for food and supplies, the rest set aside to pay our crew. Then there'd be the cost of traveling across Australia. A sense of urgency flooded through me. There had to be a way to get into the safe! Maybe, I thought—or desperately hoped—a bit of magic that had flowed through the house could be conjured again. Perhaps, as in the past, a surge of glittering mist might whisk around the knob, rotating it back and forth in exactly the correct increments. I waited, frozen, hand poised over the dial.

Nothing. No tingle of energy, no sparkle of light.

For a moment the ship felt different to me. Empty. Lifeless. Could it be the magic that had previously transformed my world was gone? That the incredible conversion of house to ship used up every ounce of the benevolent supernatural force that had saved us? A sudden chill swept through me. I supposed I'd always assumed that the mystical phenomena would be our insurance on this voyage. A manifestation of Mother and Father's love. Without it, would we survive at sea?

A conversation above roused me from these dark musings. Marni, Walter, and another voice, vaguely familiar, that caused my heart to trip. Father? I thought, in spite of myself. But no, how foolish. The tone, like Father's, was authoritative, confident, cordial. I slipped the treasured note cards into my pocket, alongside my flute, and retraced my steps up to the main deck.

I squinted into the bright sunshine and headed in the direction of the exchange. Suddenly Georgie's head popped up from behind a mountain of crates, his eyes round and wide. In agitation, he repeatedly pointed his thumb over his shoulder, the index finger of his other hand pressed over his lips. When I got closer, he lunged forward and yanked me into hiding beside him.

"It's *him*!" he whispered. "The man with the boots!"

I hunkered down and peered around the parcels. Though his back was to us, the voice was now unmistakable, as were his well-tailored jacket and sharp black boots.

"A fine vessel you have here," he said. "And newly refurbished, by the looks of it. Where did you say she was built?"

Georgie and I exchanged a look. But Walter didn't

miss a beat. "By an old-timer, upcoast, originally from Liverpool, he was. An expert craftsman with an eye for detail." As if in response, the ship creaked against the pilings, producing a sound like wry laughter—*Eeeee . . . eeeee . . . eee*—Liverpool, indeed!

"Never seen a ship quite like it," the man continued. "As graceful as a schooner, but reminiscent of a half-brig. A petite clipper ship, double-masted." He eyed the ship, fore to aft. "Peculiar features throughout. Why in the high seas would a shipbuilder place such an ornately carved door to the companionway? Looks like a drawing-room door to me! And the stained-glass window! Highly unusual."

"In fact, completely unique . . . and fast," Marni said. "I can guarantee you've never sailed anything like her before, nor will you ever again. She practically flies over the waves. And due to her streamlined design and . . ." Marni hesitated, obviously searching for the right words. ". . . exceptional performance capabilities, we won't need a very large crew. . . ."

For a few moments their talk was carried off by the breeze. I could see Marni questioning him but could not discern her words. Then the direction of the wind changed and whipped scraps of his response back to us. "Skippered . . . many a ship . . . large commercial vessels . . . voyages around the world . . . available . . ."

"Oh no!" I whispered.

"You don't think he'd be a good skipper?" Georgie asked.

"It's not that. . . ." My mind raced. He knew not one secret, but two—that we'd nearly been kidnapped, and after reading that newspaper account he'd surely surmised that we were somehow connected to the reported account of our extraordinary launching.

Georgie's eyebrows formed two high arcs. "But he was nice to us, wasn't he?"

"Yes," I murmured. And he was—but there was still something that made me uncomfortable. If he believed what he'd read, why would he want to join us?

No sooner did the thought occur to me than the question sprang from Marni's lips. "What draws you to this?—admittedly a less profitable endeavor than you're accustomed to."

I inched closer, positioning myself to the side of the crate where I could see and hear better.

He looked out to sea and back, his face suddenly pensive. "I think you'll understand me when I say this—because I read the same thing in your eyes. Some of us go to sea, not for monetary gain, but because we're drawn there. Searching for what we've lost that can never really be found. Perhaps in hope of finding something to fill that space." My heart skipped a beat. Yes, I understood that.

Marni, momentarily taken aback, quickly composed herself. I wondered what chord his words had struck in her. "If I may ask, what is it you've lost, Cap'n, and what are you searching for that cannot be found?"

He hesitated, a pained look transforming his handsome features. "Let us just say that after returning from my last voyage, I came home to discover a great loss. A shock from which I thought I might never recover. It's not something I speak of easily."

Marni gently raised her hand. "Enough said. I certainly didn't mean to pry."

"I stayed ashore for a year," the capt'n continued. "But the sea is my balm."

Marni fingered the locket at her throat. "I'm sorry for your loss, whatever it was. And I understand better than you know."

Capt'n Adams cleared his throat and went on. "This would be a welcome change of pace . . . and I admire the vessel, as I've said. It would do my heart good to be surrounded by a more genteel group of shipmates, to assist in getting you where you need to go—to be motivated by something more altruistic than getting grain and fuel to market."

The tone had changed—all business again.

Marni nodded. "And a crew?"

"At least six able-bodied seamen, besides myself . . . plus the first mate, second mate, cabin boy, and cook . . ."

Georgie shot up like a jack-in-the-box. "Marni said *I* could be the first mate!"

Marni, Walter, and the gentleman sailor turned to stare as the parcel on top of the pile teetered and fell with a thud, revealing our hiding place.

"Well, what do we have here?" the skipper asked, one eyebrow raised.

Marni held me in a serious gaze—a cautionary look that I hoped would register with Georgie before he blurted something unfortunate.

"Just playing hide-and-seek," I said, "right, Georgie?"

"I say," the skipper said. "This lad might make a good first mate! And, of course, a ship cannot sail without a cabin boy!" He smiled, his blue eyes crinkling, and extended a hand. "Captain Obediah Adams," he said. "Pleased to make your acquaintance."

As Georgie and I stepped forward, Father's ship's bell began to ring furiously, as it often had back at our house. Captain Adams turned in the direction of the clanging and stared at the persistent toller.

"It does that all by itself," Georgie explained.

The captain glanced back just as I poked Georgie with my elbow. Addie and Annie must have heard the racket as well and strolled toward us. "My family," Marni said, vaguely gesturing toward all of us.

I looked from the captain to Marni and back. Captain Obediah Adams turned a bit and winked as we shook hands. Gratefully, he was not going to mention how he'd saved us earlier. At least not yet. Maybe I should come clean and tell Marni myself. But everything inside me resisted.

"Well then, Captain," Marni said, "so you know, my family and I have the sea in our blood and will be actively involved in the sailing of this vessel. Keep that in mind when gathering a capable crew. No one given to drink or brawling. Bring them to me and I'll decide if they're suitable. We have a long voyage ahead of us and there's no time to waste. It's hurricane season as well. I'll assemble the necessary paperwork and additional supplies we'll need."

"Splendid," he said, his eyes smiling. "Happy to make your acquaintances. I'll return by afternoon, say four o'clock." Captain Adams made a courtly bow and turned on his heel. His boots clicked across the deck timbers. I watched them disappear across the gangplank.

"And who was that bonny man?" Addie asked playfully. "Quite handsome, he was, in that dandy jacket and boots! How'd ye find the likes of 'im?"

"Came by admiring the ship," Marni replied, "and we struck up a conversation. He was quite knowledgeable. Doesn't seem the superstitious sort to be rattled by rumors of specter ships, magic, and the like. We'll see what he delivers when he returns." Marni looked out to sea, fingered the silver locket at her throat, and continued. "But now we need to stow our supplies, and take stock of what we'll still be needing." She glanced about, her lively, sea-green eyes missing nothing. "Lucy, stay here with the boys and keep an eye on Annie. A nap would do you all a world of good. Addie and I need to stock the slop chest . . . oilskins, woolen drawers, denims and overalls, handkerchiefs, socks in a variety of sizes. Blankets. Caps and gloves . . ."

I was suddenly too tired to argue. A deep fatigue was already setting in. After all we'd withstood back in Maine, sailing straight through the night without so much as a wink of sleep, and then throwing ourselves directly into the new day—Marni was right. I nodded, stifling a yawn with the back of my hand.

"Let's pick our sleeping quarters," I suggested. "Come on!"

I led Annie and the boys belowdeck, and we selected our cabins—Walter and Georgie in one,

Annie and me in the other. The rooms were snug and inviting, the beds built in against the interior wall painted the same shade of robin's-egg blue as my room at home. Opposite the bunks were beautifully constructed supply cabinets and drawers with brass fittings, as well as a tall cubby for hanging clothing. Light shone in from a single porthole set between the cabinetry. In the middle of the cabin a large hammock hung, strung wall to wall.

Annie scrambled to the top berth and curled up like a contented kitten. Pugsley hopped into the lower compartment with me. I stretched out, punched and fluffed my pillow, flipped onto my side, and drew up my knees. Ah . . . it would be good to rest! But something pressed against my hip. I rolled onto my back and my hand went to my pocket, removing my treasures—my flute, father's cuff links, the box of tacks, pencil, and stationery. These I carefully placed on the wooden shelf along the wall beside my bunk and resituated myself in my cozy nest. I pulled the patchwork quilt Mother had stitched for me up to my chin, but, try as I might, I could not sleep. In spite of Annie's gentle snoring, and Pugsley's wheezy breathing beside me, I felt totally alone. I lay there in the dim-lit cabin, staring at the ceiling, counting worries the way others count sheep. I yawned again and again, until my eyes were bleary. Still, my mind raced.

Finally I sat up, took the pencil and a piece of Mother's stationery. "Mother," I whispered. "I'm scared. . . ." I grasped the stub of pencil in my sweaty hand and printed across the top of the page: *WORRIES:*

Perhaps if I wrote them all out they would stop plaguing me.

1. *Captain Adams might tell Marni about the attempted kidnapping.*
2. *The authorities might ask for our ship's registration and passenger manifest—that we don't have!*
3. *I don't know how to sail, not really!*
4. *We might hit a tropical storm—or WORSE, a hurricane.*
5. *What if the crew isn't capable?*
6. *What if we run out of food? Or someone gets sick at sea?*

I continued, additional what-ifs marching across my brain. It was as though by releasing one worry, I'd dispatched a whole army of them!

7. *When (if?!) we get to Australia, how will we find Aunt Pru?*
8. *What if we run out of money?*

True, we had the satchel of loot from the judge—his crooked payment for the house, intended for Uncle Victor. But how long would that last? My thoughts returned to Father's safe. Perhaps it held not only money, stocks and bonds and the like, but—who knew?—might it hold a clue to Aunt Pru's whereabouts? I picked up the pencil again and continued to scrawl my concerns.

9. *What if I can't open the safe?*
10. *What if the magic is gone forever?*

The next what-if was too frightening to write down, as if putting it to paper would add to its power. Try as I might, the worry wouldn't leave me. . . . What if, I thought, what if we don't find Aunt Pru? What if the rumors of a family curse are true and we're lost at sea, just like Father and his father before him? Just like Mother? What if the magic that brought us this far was all just a part of the curse—luring us far out on the ocean, where we'll be swallowed up and forgotten?

As the horrible thought took root and grew in my mind, I crumbled my worry list and heaved it at the wall as the ship's bell began to clang yet again.

4

It was late afternoon when I rose from my nap, greeted with a savory-sweet smell—a chowder or seafood stew. My mouth watered and stomach rumbled. Pugsley stirred and stretched out his front paws, hindquarters raised. His little black nose twitched at the aroma wafting into the cabin. In an instant he leaped from my berth, claws clicking along the polished, wooden-planked floor.

I sat up, disoriented for a moment. Yes, this was *my* cabin, *my* berth, belowdecks on *my* ship. Yes, Annie was asleep in the bunk above me—except, when I stood I saw that her covers were thrown back and the bed was empty. I headed into the companionway, past the stateroom, and on toward the seductive smell beckoning from the galley.

There, in the middle of the low-ceilinged room, stood a small cast-iron woodstove, an array of sparkling pots and pans hanging above it. Dusky sun streamed through a small skylight, casting a wide beam on a table of hardwood riveted to the floor, with a lip all the way around the edge. Long benches were anchored along each side of the table. One of Mother's copper pots bubbled merrily on the stovetop, and as I stepped into the narrow galley, I spied the backside of someone crouched before a built-in cupboard. I stopped short as the figure rolled back on his heels and stood.

He was at least six feet tall, thin and wiry as a broomstick. The fellow's tightly braided hair nearly skimmed the ceiling. His denim work pants and blousy muslin shirt were covered with a white apron. I didn't mean to stare, but I'd never seen skin so black and smooth. The man's long lean face shone like a polished onyx stone. Pugsley sat beside him, his buggy eyes roaming from the pot, to the man, to me, and back again.

"Well, den, pleased t' make your 'quaintance, missy," he said, wiping his hands on his apron. "Rasjohnny, I em. Cap'n Adams fetched me 'ere t' cook up some tasty fare."

My hand flew to my head—I'd forgotten my cap! My curls must have burst free as I slept. Too late now, and after all, I couldn't keep up the charade forever, could I? Rasjohnny had already turned, wielding a large spoon, and stirred the pot with several vigorous strokes. Pugsley's ears perked up at each clank and swish. The man leaned in and sniffed. "Ah yes, sweet 'n' saucy! Jerk cod and mussels—scallops too! Lobster. Shrimp. Taste?"

"Ummmm! Me too!"

I turned in the direction of the singsongy voice to find myself face-to-face with a boy a few years older than Georgie—a miniature version of the cook, except that his skin was the color of coffee with cream, his eyes riveting hazel orbs that sparkled like gold. He picked up a spoon, stepped to the pot, scooped, slurped, and offered me the rest. "Wanna try?"

"Javan!" Rasjohnny barked. "You think dis li'l lady want t'eat from dat utensil dere? Use some o'dat brain power, how 'bout it?" Rasjohnny poked the air with his own spoon. "Dis my son, Javan. Who most often knows what polite looks like. Go dip dat spoon in da dishpan, Javan, go on!"

Javan shrugged and did as he was told. "What's your name, miss?" he called over his shoulder.

"Lucy." My stomach let out a cavernous growl. Rasjohnny grinned. "The sea'll do dat, yessiree!" He lifted a thick white bowl from a column stacked in a wooden slatted holder mounted on the wall. In one flourish, he ladled a stream of chunky stew, equipped me with an oversize spoon, and dropped a hunk of bread on top.

"Swab it up right, and tell Rasjohhny dat ain't da best spicy seafood y' ever et!"

As I carried my bowl to the galley table, Walter and Georgie appeared. Javan nodded a greeting. Apparently they'd already met.

"Grab y'selfs a bowl," Rasjohnny called. "Yessir! Boys, de alw'ys got an app'tite!"

In minutes Walter and Georgie, then Annie and Addie were seated with me, knee to knee, around the table. Marni held her bowl in hand and ate standing in the doorway. *Slurp* and *clink*, *ooh* and *ah*. Pugsley scratched at my shin and whined. The stew was tangy, spicy, with hints of cinnamon and allspice, maybe brown sugar. Rasjohnny looked on, smiling, ladle at the ready to dish out seconds. Javan sat atop a water barrel beside the stove, expertly devouring his stew with only the help of a hunk of bread. Georgie made a big show of not looking at the cook's son, except when he raised his eyes and watched from beneath a forehead full of hair. Javan, on the other hand, studied all of us, his amber eyes sweeping the room as he ate.

Annie wiped her mouth with the back of her hand. "And Mr. Johnny brought a goat and some chickens too! It'll be my job to look after them!"

"Fresh milk 'n' eggs," Rasjohnny declared. "Yessir, way tasty out on da water! Javan'll teach ya how to milk da li'l nanny. Nuttin' to it!"

Our eyes all rose to the sound of footfall on the stairs. I knew even before I spotted the black boots who the commanding steps belonged to.

"I take it everyone is duly impressed with the culinary skill of my associates here?"

Addie slipped out of the bench and stood before him. "A fine meal, it 'tis," she said, dabbing her mouth demurely with her napkin. She tipped her head, blue eyes twinkling. "And, sir, sometimes a kitchen needs a woman's touch, 'tis true! What with milk an' eggs, I'd be happy t' whip up somethin' that'd bring a smile to yer lips! "

Marni's eyes widened and Addie wilted under her gaze, cheeks reddening. She quickly slid back to her place at table. Captain Adams cleared his throat. "Well then . . . yes," he stammered, a slight blush creeping across his face. "I say, Miss Marni, when you finish your meal I've some crewmen for you to meet. Up on the poop deck then, when you've had your fill?"

Grunts and nods all around as our spoons scraped the last of the tasty Caribbean concoction. With our bread we sponged up what was left, leaving the bowls nearly sparkling. We stacked our dishes and headed through the companionway, and Marni, Walter, and I climbed upstairs to the main deck. The sun shone low in the sky and we were greeted by the sounds of men calling out, gulls crying, the clatter of metal-clad wheels rumbling over cobble and wood.

Leaning along the rail were two men, one small and wiry with a sharp, possum-like face. His right eye was cloudy and rolled to the side, giving him a restless air. The other was a big, broad young man with massive arms and a thick neck. His features seemed lost in the doughy flesh of his face. One was as small and quick as the other large and slow. Captain Adams strode toward us.

"Grady! Quaide!" he barked, and the unlikely pair straightened up, somewhat resentfully, it seemed to me. The large one took a long drag on a cigarette before flicking it overboard. The diminutive older man adjusted his overalls and straightened his flat-topped cap. "Miss Marni," the captain began, "these two men have, collectively, circled the world many times aboard ships large and small. Two more capable sailors you will never find. Grady here . . ." He paused, gesturing toward the slight seaman. "Grady will be my first mate—works the rigging like nobody I've seen—fearless, he is—can spring like a squirrel amongst the masts, climb the ropes like a spider in its web."

Grady, thin lipped and frowning, nodded his head in acknowledgment. I noticed his one good eye scrutinizing me, then Marni, then Pugsley, who'd scampered upstairs behind us.

"And Quaide here—he's a workhorse of a second mate. Can lift and hoist like a machine, and, when necessary, defend a vessel against any threat." Quaide jutted out his chin and rolled his shoulders, hands twitching by his sides. The man's small, beady eyes shifted from side to side, avoiding direct contact with any of us. I disliked him immediately and glanced at Marni to gauge her reaction. As Marni studied him, I saw that mysterious faraway look in her eyes that I knew so well—seeing something the rest of us couldn't. I shifted my gaze from Marni to Walter, hoping he'd see what I saw in the man. But Walter only nodded in grudging admiration of Quaide's ample biceps.

"And then, the rest of the crew . . ." Cap'n Adams whistled sharply through his teeth and raised a hand. A motley bunch sauntered aboard, all them embodying the swagger associated with the rolling of a ship. Mostly they looked down, but each cast a curious glance at our assembled group.

"These two here—Red and Red," the cap'n said, waving toward a set of identical twins, tall and gangly, high foreheads surrounded by a frizz of carrot-red hair. They were older than they appeared at first glance—perhaps in their thirties, their white skin peppered with freckles. The cap'n shrugged. "That's what they go by. Red and Red. Work together like a hand in a glove."

"Aye, aye," they answered, grinning matched, gap-toothed smiles.

"And this is Irish," Cap'n Obediah continued. "Black Irish, they say, isn't that right?"

A ruddy-complexioned man with dark eyes and curly jet-black hair nodded. "'Tis true," he said. "Me colorin' comes from the Conquistadors plantin' their seeds on the green isle! Got the luck o' the Irish, the fire of the Spaniards."

"Tonio . . ." Cap'n Adams pointed, and a stocky man with a bald shiny head stepped forward, expressionless. A thick black mustache covered his top lip, the ends waxed into curling points. Angry eyebrows met in the middle above the wide bridge of his nose. "Comes from Venice—a descendant of Marco Polo, right, Tonio?"

Tonio shrugged. "*Sono un marinaio regulare,*"

he said, "a regular sailor."

"Just a joke," the cap'n answered. Clearly Tonio didn't have much of a sense of humor, so the cap'n went on. "And last but not least, Coleman . . ." Cap'n extended a hand toward an older fellow with creased and weathered skin, and arms too long for his body. The thin crop of hair that blew about his head was surely once blond, now a nameless bland hue, streaked with gray. Even Coleman's blue eyes seemed faded, as did the large tattoo on his right forearm of a buxom mermaid. Walter stared, open-mouthed, until Marni poked him. "Better men you'll never find," the cap'n reassured. I sized them up, one to the next. I hoped the cap'n was right—that this was the group that could guide us safely to Aunt Pru.

Marni assessed them all through squinting eyes. Finally she spoke. "We will run a tight ship. My family is aboard. There'll be no drinking, curs-ing, or gambling. We will work together as a team. Is that clear?"

"Yes, ma'am," they mumbled.

"Have any of you sailed around the Cape of Good Hope?"

"I 'ave," Grady said. "Many times. It's danger-ous. But," he added a little too quickly, "it can be done. I'm up fer it."

"Aye aye," Quaide said, his voice thick and grainy as oatmeal.

"Captain has discussed your pay and you find the terms acceptable?"

"Yes, missus."

Walter asked, "How soon can you leave?"

"Soon as I fetch me ditty bag," Grady said.

"Yeah," Quaide added. Red's and Red's heads bobbed enthusiastically. The others grunted their assent. I watched Quaide slip toward the back of the group. For a large man he had a way of moving that seemed designed not to draw attention to itself.

"What questions do you have for us?" Walter asked with an air of confidence. Quaide tilted his head toward the Reds and mouthed, "Kinda young to be so sure of hisself, ain't he?" Glancing Walter's way, I suddenly saw my friend through a stranger's eyes. It had not occurred to me how standing in for his father had prepared him for this. Capable. Responsible. He met my gaze with a quizzical look. I quickly turned my attention back to the seamen.

Grady shifted uncomfortably. "There's rumors about," he began. "A specter ship, with a group aboard—a siren, and a bunch o' kids." As if on cue, Georgie and Annie burst through the doorway and slid across the deck in a game of chase, Pugsley yipping at their heels, Addie behind them. "Seems a bit of a coincidence." His one good eye darted between us. Rasjohnny and Javan appeared, joining the others.

It seemed my heart might hammer right through my chest. Marni's expression never changed. "I've known seafarers to be a superstitious lot, and newspapermen play on that to sell papers. We've seen the hastily written news story. Objective journalism, it isn't!" She placed a hand on my shoulder. "What's true is this—the young lady in the newspaper account is none other than our Lucy here. Alive and well." I felt the curious eyes of the sailors ogling me and forced myself to meet their gazes straight on. One by one they looked away. "And," Marni continued, gesturing toward Walter and his siblings, "the Perkins children. If you believe everything you read, I must be the siren." With that, she tapped both feet. "Does that look like a mermaid's tail to any of you? See any fins? Scales?"

Captain Adams chuckled. The group of them gahuffed. Rasjohnny grinned and Javan sized each of us up. Old Grady still looked doubtful. Quaide chewed the inside of his cheek, his fleshy face a blank slab.

"Fact is," Marni continued, "as is often the case, at least part of the news story is true. Yes, there was a freak hurricane, and yes, the Simmons mansion was washed out to sea. These children escaped the disaster, and with no place to call home, we decided to leave the painful memories behind." She looked them each in the eye, one to the other. "And after reading the account of Jeremiah Perkins, you can see why they need a more stable environment. Miss Addie is along to offer additional support." Addie nodded, hazel eyes sparkling.

Grady's gray eyebrows wiggled up and down like a pair of hairy caterpillars. He bit his lower lip.

"If you have any doubts or worries, you're not the man for the job," Walter said. His confidence bolstered my spirit. How handsome he looked. How capable!

"And," Marni added, "you can see why we need to set sail sooner rather than later. Last thing we want is a throng of curiosity seekers traipsing by. These children have been through enough already."

"Me—I'm in," Quaide said. "I don't take no account o' nonsense."

Grady repeatedly rubbed his index finger to thumb, as if polishing away his worry. "You been at sea long as I 'ave, you learn not to take its mysteries lightly. But awright . . . I'm trustin' there won't be no peculiarities, so t' speak."

Rasjohnny piped in, "Javan and me—we's in from da get-go."

The rest of them—the two Reds, Tonio, Irish, and Coleman—nodded in agreement.

"That's it then," Marni said. "Tomorrow, or at

the latest the next day, we depart. Gather what you need and report at daybreak. There's much to be done!"

Grady looked off into the sunset, which cast an orange glow across his face. A ghost of a full moon hung in the evening sky like a distant silver coin. "Today . . . Tuesday," he said, thinking aloud, calculating the days on gnarled fingers. "Tomorrow . . . Wednesday—the luckiest day of all to set sail. Full moon t'night. High tide at dawn. Bodes well, it does. That's when we should leave, Miss Marni. Tomorrow. All the signs are right. To wait until Thursday . . ." He vigorously shook his head. "Bad luck." The ship's bell began to toll. "Y'see?" Grady said. "A portend. Warning us t'set sail at mornin' time. Tomorrow."

Marni scanned the odd collection of mariners. "Let's see if the morning finds us ready. Do what you need to do this evening. All of you."

Our prospective crew agreed and loped toward the gangplank.

"One more thing," Marni said, stopping them in their tracks, pointing from one to the other. "Not a word to anyone about this ship or that newspaper drivel. Your lips are sealed, understood?"

"Yes, ma'am," they replied, but, it seemed to me, without much conviction.

5

I awoke the next day before dawn—not even a thin trace of daylight showing through the porthole. Annie was still breathing in the steady rhythm of sleep, and Pugsley, curled in my bunk, was snoring. Clearly, neither of them was troubled by vexing anxieties of any kind. My thoughts turned to Mother and Father—to Aunt Pru—and feelings of grief and loneliness swirled around me. So strong was the current of these emotions that I felt I might drown in them. I sighed. My feelings were so like the sea—how quickly they could turn from calm to stormy. From confident to sad.

This was not the proper state of mind in which to embark on our voyage! I dangled my legs over the edge of the hammock and swung it back until my feet touched the floor. One thing I could thank my late Uncle Victor for was this—he'd taught me that the best medicine for self-pity was hard work. Not his, but mine.

I got up, pulled on my denims, and tied my sturdy work boots with double knots. As if affirming my intent, I suddenly heard the muffled sounds of voices above. Hurried steps on deck. The shuffle and drag of supplies being moved. Good. There would be plenty to do if we were going to set sail today. And much to learn. What with the threat of the curse, along with the usual challenges of the sea, I was bound and determined to become the best sailor I could be. It's what Father would have expected.

I walked through the narrow corridor, my hand skimming the smooth polished banister, and paused outside the chart room. After a moment's hesitation I slipped inside. The collection of Father's seafaring paraphernalia bolstered my spirits further. Hastily I picked up his fine brass spyglass and hung it around my neck. It would be fun to watch the Boston waterfront fade as we sailed out of the harbor. Without further delay I scaled the narrow stairs to the main deck.

Marni nodded a good morning. The captain stood amidst the carefully coiled lines and folded canvas. Grady, Quaide, and Walter moved and adjusted what would become the means of our wind power. The Reds scaled the yardarms, and Tonio and Irish hauled crates and barrels, then neatly coiled the thick lines waiting to be called upon when needed. Rasjohnny, too, moved deftly from task to task, humming under his breath. Marni knelt beside Addie, guiding her able hands along carefully folded and wrapped sheets of sail. I took my place, pointedly ignoring the look of disdain on Quaide's face, and concentrated on working twice as hard and fast without complaint. I would make Father proud and force Quaide to swallow his unspoken scorn. As I worked, tugging, folding, tucking, my eye traveled past the trestletrees, spars, and yardarms that stood perpendicular to the masts, the complex system of rigging and ratlines running between them. Once we set sail, we would all be taking a watch, sometimes up in the crow's nest platform at the highest point aloft. My heart thrilled, while my knees went weak. Excitement and trepidation, all rolled into one.

The sun was climbing the horizon, a layer of molten gold over the water. Walter caught my eye, smiled, and gave me a thumbs-up. I grinned back, delighted I had apparently passed this first test. "Not bad for a girl," Grady added, staring at me from beneath his ample brows. He pronounced *girl* in two syllables: "goy-el."

The cap'n said, "Nice job!" The Reds nodded. Marni looked at me with an expression that said, "Told you so." And my spirits soared.

The aroma of coffee and frying bacon and eggs drew us to the galley, all but Quaide, who had, he said, "some last-minute dealings onshore." He would have to be quick about it—already, on our starboard side, a stocky little tugboat readied herself to tow us on an ebb tide out of the harbor, until we could hoist sail and let the wind take us. And there was Javan, pressing bacon in the cast-iron skillet until crisp and brown and ably flipping eggs from pan to plate. This he did with the flair of a vaudevillian, much to Annie's delight. I wolfed down my breakfast as Javan watched, puffed with pride. Each of us rinsed our plates and stacked them back in their proper place. Rasjohnny kept the coffee hot, declaring, "Java all day 'n' night, come as you need it!"

Ahead of the rest, I ran back through the companionway up to the poop deck and leaned over the rail. Early as it was, the pier was abuzz with activity. I squinted through Father's spyglass, and the scene became magnified, the faces of pass-ersby suddenly intimate, their lips forming words I could not hear. I studied the wharf, wondering where this stern man was going, or what that stout woman was laughing about. I swept a glance right, then left, a sudden surprise close-up of someone's nose or ear requiring me to extend or retract the telescope. Unknowingly, people found themselves under inspection. Back and forth, I examined each shorefront pedestrian.

A handsome woman in a stylish frock strolled along—something in her carriage reminded me of Mother. I adjusted the focus and drank in the sight of her, training the lens on her every move, follow-ing her graceful steps in an easterly direction.

Suddenly, something peculiar happened. It was as though the tubular device took on a will of its own. Instead of continuing to keep the woman in my sight, some unseen power drew the scope in the opposite direction, as if guided by an invisible iron grasp. Frustrated as I was at the stubborn force that guided the spyglass, my heart thrilled—the magic! Was it back? I attempted to adjust the focal point at the woman, but no. I decided to cooperate, and the imperceptible energy shifted my aim toward the west.

"What is it?" I exclaimed. As if in response, my

eye was drawn back to the ocular cup like metal to magnet. The scope fairly buzzed in my hands. Of its own accord it telescoped in and out, finally bringing a small crowd of people into focus. Closer and closer, until all that filled my lens was an eye, an arresting translucent shade of green—the color of sea glass. Then the spyglass telescoped out, the eye assuming its place in the face of a man in khaki-colored trousers and shirt, his lips moving in conversation.

To the left of the green-eyed man, a fleshy white face and thick neck jumped into view. It was Quaide. A look of concentration creased the width of his forehead. He gestured toward our ship with a beefy hand. Another companion to his right set my heart racing. Even though it was only the back of his head, he was unmistakable. Just as before, his greasy hair straggled from beneath the red bandana. He nodded and shot a glance over his shoulder. The raised scar slithered crossways over his cheek like a purple snake. Quaide thumped the scoundrel on the back. The green-eyed man nodded and withdrew a wad of money from his pocket. He counted out two, three, five, ten bills into each of their outstretched hands. Quaide stuffed the money into his pocket and began walking toward our ship. Scarface and the green-eyed man went the opposite way. So engrossed was I in this observation that I never heard approaching steps behind me. A blunt blow to my backside threw me into the rail.

I spun around and was confronted by a scrappy brown-and-white creature, stomping its cloven, hoofed feet and playfully ducking its head. Annie ran up alongside. "Lucy, meet my goat! Look! She has blue eyes!"

"We've already met," I said, rubbing my sore behind. The little goat tipped her head side to side and regarded me quizzically. She did have lovely sky-blue eyes with black elongated pupils.

"Baaaaaaaaa." Her short turned-up tail twitched and wagged.

"I named her Ida," Annie said. "She knows her name. Ida! Ida!" The small sure-footed creature scrambled up a set of steps to a perch at the highest point on deck and looked back at us. "Baaaaa."

I turned away from this distraction and put my scope to eye, hoping to catch Quaide in my lens again. But the peculiar energy that had directed the scope was gone. The sound of Annie's excited chatter faded as I concentrated on the shore—this man, that fellow—no . . . no . . . I did manage to pinpoint the scoundrel in the red bandana, walking swiftly away on bowed legs, the green-eyed man beside him. I followed their progress in and out of the throngs, making their way toward the gangway of another ship. My eyes began to ache, the left from being pressed shut, the right from peering into the eyepiece. Sounds behind me finally drew my attention and I put down the lens.

There was Quaide, moving seamlessly back into the rhythm of the work at hand. He never looked up, and made no sound. Unless one was particularly observant, he might never have been missed.

The tugboat beside us sounded its horn in three honking blasts. Cap'n Adams called out above it, "All hands! All hands on deck!" I watched as the crew manned various stations. My job, along with Addie, was to keep Georgie and Annie safe and out of harm's way. I did my part, with Georgie hankering to join the others and Annie fussing over her rambunctious little goat. This was not work suitable for a sea cap'n's daughter, I thought resentfully. I followed, with keen interest, the way the seamen worked like parts of a well-oiled machine—lines being tied and untied, winches creaking and straining, the raising of the anchor, sails at the ready.

"All-a-taut," the cap'n hollered. "All-a-taut, and ready to go!"

The ship's bell clanged, announcing our departure. As we navigated through the busy harbor with Cap'n Adams at the helm I made a vow—this would be the last time I stood by as a passive observer. A sailor I would become, like my father and his father before him. I was a Simmons, after all!

The shorefront faded until it became a distant blur on the horizon. Grady, Quaide, Irish, and Coleman had climbed the ratlines to the trestletree platforms, and there, hauled, swayed, and hoisted her sails. With a whip and a snap, each sheet, in turn, caught the wind. "Steady on!" the cap'n shouted. "Steady on!" A slap and a jolt as still another sail swelled. Her masts and timbers creaked in cooperation. The sea tumbled and foamed as her bow cut through the waves, sending a brilliant torrent of ocean spray around the figurehead and bowsprit.

I pulled my flute from my pocket. It hummed in my hands, as if trembling at the thrill of the moment. I put it to my lips and the tune Father had taught me cascaded into the sea air. *A la dee dah dah . . . a la dee dah dee!* In response, Father's bell began to clang, and a crying gull swooped low overhead. The hints of magic bolstered my confidence, and, for a moment, all thoughts of family curses and litanies of worries were carried off with the wind. I imagined my aunt, being swept up in her arms, and then, the two of us piecing together the pieces of our family puzzle.

I closed my eyes as the salty mist kissed my face. Aunt Pru, I said to myself, we're on our way!

6

The first week at sea provided an education like none I'd experienced before: learning by doing, then doing some more. Never had I worked so hard, and slept so soundly, braced and bolstered by the sharp salt air in my lungs, the wind in my hair. I had little time to ruminate on worries—there was too much to be done!

The difficult responsibilities we learned first, in order to ensure that when we hit the more challenging legs of our journey our crew would be fully prepared. And that meant learning to climb to the highest point of the rigging, the royal yard. Over one hundred feet up it was, and what with the bobbing and swaying of the ship, a challenge that could never be taken lightly. Grady and Quaide scoffed at my insistence on being included in this lesson. The Reds shook their heads in tandem. Irish spoke up, "Why worry yourself with this, miss? It's mighty dangerous, it is!" The cap'n, too, expressed his view that such a task was better left to the men. Their warnings both frightened me and, at the same time, fed my determination to prove them wrong. Marni seemed to understand my need to conquer this, to contribute fully, and with no more than the intensity of her gaze and a nod of her head she somehow calmed the anxieties of the rest.

As in all things, Walter paved the way, swallowing any fear and trepidation. I watched him move methodically along the ladder-like ratlines, through the four levels of sails, grasping rope, and the wooden deadeyes that held the shrouds in place. Javan climbed in tandem with him, along the opposite mast. Up, up to the main yard and on to the trestletree above it. My heart thumped as his foot slipped from the rope and he hung for a moment like a monkey on a vine. Only when he wrapped his arm around the mast, and pumped air with his feet until he connected again, did my breath return.

Grady followed behind him like a nimble squirrel, barking directions. Quaide stood below, arms folded, waiting, it seemed, for Walter to flounder. The Reds passed by quickly, looking up, nodding and grinning their approval. Tonio, Irish, and Coleman paid him no mind, just continued to go about their business.

"Yes, Walter!" I shouted, fist in the air. "Almost there!"

He continued toward the topsail, and paused at the trestletree closest to the topgallant spar. Watching him was enough to turn my stomach queasy. The higher he went, the more he would feel the sway of the ship, the farther he'd tumble if he lost a hand- or foothold. And beneath all of these fears was the realization that I would be next.

Still Walter inched upward, Grady a ways behind him, to the spar of the royal yard—about one hundred twenty feet above the deck! By now an audience had assembled—Marni watching calmly, Addie wringing her hands, Georgie grinning ear to ear, and Annie, a clucking chicken tucked under each arm.

Walter, hanging on with one hand, threw his cap in the air as he reached the highest point. His shout of triumph sounded a million miles away, and I wondered if he could hear our applause. His descent was quicker than the climb, or maybe it just seemed that way because it meant my moment of reckoning was that much closer.

He jumped from about eight feet up, landing soundly in front of me, his face alight with excitement and pride. Before I knew what was happening I was enclosed in a bear hug, my face pressed into the hollow of his neck. He squeezed me tight, lifted me off the ground, and spun me around once, twice, before depositing me back on deck.

"Wait till you try! Nothing like it, Lucy!" he cried, beaming.

Without even a moment to recover—my face still burning, insides turned to mush at Walter's embrace—Grady was beside me. "Now or never, miss," he uttered, his lips barely moving, eyes not meeting mine. He raised his pointy chin toward the ratlines, indicating where I was to begin. Javan, too, called out to me, pointing a *V* of fingers between my eyes and his. "Ya look only across—not up, not down—just here. Opposite ya I'll be, far's I can go!" As if by silent agreement the rest gathered—Coleman, always the loner, off to one side, elbows resting on the rail; the two Reds sitting aft atop the poop deck; Irish leaning against the shrouds; and Tonio standing like a rock out on the upper fo'c'sle deck.

"Go on!" Walter encouraged.

Instead of stepping forward I became a statue, as solid and unmoving as the figurehead of my aunt and uncle reaching out over the waves. My mouth went dry as dead leaves, my palms damp and slippery as jellyfish. A gull soared overhead and dropped a clam onto the deck, shattering its shell and exposing its innards. I flinched. That could be me—a splat on the timbers. The rocking of the ship, the force of the wind, the height of the masts all taunted me. The gull swooped down and picked the clam clean. I shuddered and felt a hand on my shoulder.

"No harm will come to you," Marni whispered. I felt her warm breath in my ear and closed my eyes. "I'm sure of it." Addie reached out and gave my hand a squeeze. As if to confirm the sentiment, the flute hummed in my pocket and the ship's bell clanged.

"On with it," Grady said.

Quaide snorted. "Nah, she ain't gonna do it!"

I opened my eyes and glared at him. Wiped my sweaty hands on my overalls, then reached for the rope, its weave rough against my fingers. Pulled. Stepped up with my right foot. Left. Left hand up, grasp. Stretch. Right over left. One foot then the other, toes groping. I felt the bounce of the rope netting bearing my weight. Reach, clasp, pull, climb.

I hardly was aware of Grady behind me. I looked only forward, not up, and certainly not down, one thought propelling me—for you, Aunt Pru! Javan climbed opposite me, making it seem easy. He and Grady would climb as far as they could to aid me. After that I'd be on my own.

I reached the trestletree at the top of the lower mast. Paused. Held tight. If I did this, I reasoned, all I'd need to do was repeat the process—three more times.

I took a deep breath and glanced aloft. The world tilted and a wave of vertigo swept over me. I tightened my grip and pressed my eyes shut, willing the swoon to pass. Look only forward, I told myself again. Straight ahead.

I began my ascent anew, refusing to stop until I reached the main yard. The world was blue and white, sky and sail, nothing more. Up, up, up to the topsail. There, the topgallant spar. I spliced my arms through the lines to my elbows, pulled my forearms to me, gripping the rope. My boots slid along the rungs to where the stocky heel caught and held. Hanging securely, I chanced a downward glance.

The deck seemed a small wooden game board, my friends and crew below, the playing pieces. The expanse of green-blue sea was endless. The wind, much stronger up here, whipped my hair across my face. With one hand I grabbed and twisted the wild locks into a single coil and shoved them into the collar of my work shirt. But the wind shifted, throwing my balance askew. Right hand and foot flailing, I clung to the ropes with only my left hand. My left foot slipped and slid, pitching me at a dangerous diagonal. A flash of ocean, then sails, then deck. I thrashed about, desperately trying to swing myself back toward the ratline.

A voice came to me, not Grady's, not Javan's or Walter's. Calm. Steady.

Easy. Don't swing with your right. Steady with your left. Anchor yourself. There. Slide your foot back to center. Yes. That's my girl. Perfect. Hug the lines with your left. Draw in with the right. Yes, just so . . .

This I did, step by step. It may have been my imagination, but it was as though the mast and the lines responded to the voice as well, suddenly cooperating with me, swelling and bending in order to meet me halfway. An uncanny calm blossomed within me. Taking a deep fortifying breath, I crept onward and upward.

I squinted into the wind. My shirt whipped and snapped about. A surge of strength and determination propelled me, and there, finally, the spar of the royal yard! I held steady. Inhaled deeply. This is how heaven must feel, why Father had loved the sea! The calm steady voice I'd heard—of course. It was Father's voice! And then the ship, the way it, too, responded to his words, the subtle benevolent movements of mast and line. They were all somehow connected—Father, our house turned ship, the magic—and this view from the crow's nest. How fortunate to have the privilege of climbing up here. I took one last look before my descent.

There, on the horizon, another ship. Or was it? I raised a hand over my brow to shield the sun. Yes. The outline of a sleek schooner came into view and out. One moment clear to me, the next blending almost invisibly into the field of blue. So fast was she traveling that she appeared to be flying above the surface of the sea. Perhaps it was the glare of the sun through the ocean spray, but now and again an aura of rainbow-colored mist seemed to envelop her. If only I had my spyglass, I thought. And there, back toward the harbor, another ship, black timbered and square-rigged, not as fast as ours, nor as graceful as the schooner. I'd recognize it anywhere—it was the vessel Georgie and I'd almost been dragged aboard back in Boston.

I felt a tug on the cuff of my dungarees—I'd forgotten all about Grady. "Are ye comin' back down, miss, or are ye gonna stay 'ere all the live-long day?"

"I'm coming!" I shouted. Walter had made

it look easy, but actually it was trickier than the upward climb, mostly because I had to lead with my feet and could not see my footholds. Stepping into air, trusting the feel of rope rungs beneath my feet, remembering not to shift weight until I felt my boot catch and hold.

Finally, when I was in jumping distance of the deck, I let go of the lines and leaped to the ground. Walter draped his arm around my shoulders and squeezed me tight. Marni smiled, her expression saying, "I knew you could do it!" Addie pulled me into an embrace as Javan hopped down beside me, both thumbs pointing up.

"Good as gold!" he shouted. "Yessiree!"

Annie clapped, releasing one frightened chicken after the other in a flurry of feathers. The rest came from their respective places, all applauding. I'd proved something here, and suddenly everything had changed.

"We're gonna name ye Red Three!" It was the first time I'd actually heard either of the Reds speak. It was high praise, for sure. I smiled and ran a hand through my own locks. Georgie shrugged. "It's not *that* big a deal," he muttered. Grady laughed and patted Georgie on the head.

"Not to worry, little guy. You'll get your turn before long!"

I shot a glance Quaide's way, my chin held a little higher, my smile a bit wider.

"Ain't as easy on the high seas," Quaide said flatly. "Or in a storm." He wiggled the toothpick between his lips in a circular motion, took it, and flicked it overboard. Spit a particle from the tip of his tongue and mopped his mouth with a fan of thick fingers. "We'll see how she fares then."

I thought of Father's voice, unruffled and confident, guiding me, step by step. Yes, I thought, watching Quaide lumber off, we'll see.

7

"Remember," Grady said, looking my way, "first watch starts at midnight. Midnight to four in the mornin'. That one's tough for a wet-behind-the-ears sailor. In this new rotation, me, Quaide, Coleman, and Tonio'll continue to take first watch. Then there's mornin' watch, four t' eight," he said, pointing to Walter. "Whaddya say?"

As Walter nodded, a thought struck me. The morning watch would include the sunrise. "I'll take that one," I said. "I don't mind waking early."

"It ain't just lookin' at the scenery," Grady said, as if reading my mind, "but all the chores that need attention."

"Have I let you down yet?"

Grady grunted an acknowledgment and reiterated each watch—forenoon, afternoon, both two-hour dog watches, and the night watch. Sleep would be rationed in four-hour stretches. Chores, or upkeep of the ship—its timbers, hardware, sails— these tasks would be constant.

"You," Grady exclaimed, taking Georgie by the shoulder. "How 'bout this week we'll try ye out as the timekeeper, markin' every half hour by the bell, one ring for each? Yer sister and Miss Addie can help." This perked Georgie up considerably. He ran to the bell to give it a ring. The rest of us dispersed, to chores, to rest, or to keep watch.

I made my way back to my cabin, needing some time alone. Besides taking my part in the inevitable washing down of the decks, chipping rust from the ironworks, coating them with red lead and white paint, pumping the bilge, and airing and repairing sails stored in the lazaret, there were my own personal tasks of another nature altogether. The first of these was to figure out how to open Father's safe and discover whatever clues it might hold that would help us locate Pru. I had a strong, inexplicable intuition that told me this was not only important, but imperative. I *had* to discover the combination!

Inside the cabin I climbed into my bunk and reached for a tablet of paper and pencil from the built-in shelf beside me. I flipped back the cover and chewed the pencil thoughtfully. The combination would be three numbers. The locking mechanism was circled in increments, from 1 to 39. I drew two vertical lines down the page, creating three columns. In the left column I wrote the number 1; in the middle column, 2; the right-hand column, 3. Then I drew a horizontal line below that first possible (though unlikely) combination. I would simply continue switching the number in the first column, increasing it each time by one. Then, I'd do the same thing with column two, and finally, column three.

Feeling quite smug at my clever systematic approach, I quickly filled thirty-nine rows and a page and a half, crossing out any combinations with duplicate numbers side by side: 1-2-3 . . . 2-2-3 . . . 3-2-3 . . . 4-2-3, and so on, until finally—39-2-3. Then I began the next group of numbers, altering just column two: 1-1-3 . . . 1-2-3 . . . 1-3-3 . . . 1-4-3 . . . all the way up to 1-39-3.

Five pages in, when I'd completed the third sequence of numbers, ending with: 1-2-39, a terrible thought occurred to me. Creating three columns of numbers, each beginning with *1*, would not be enough! Hitting upon *every* possible combination—such as 39-17-20—would require that I create three combinations beginning with *each* number from 1 to 39! Suddenly it was apparent that the variety of combinations was seemingly infinite. In frustration (and embarrassed at my initial foolish optimism), I grabbed hold of my futile scrawlings, tore them from the book, and crumpled them into a ball.

But wait.

I'd spent the time and there were, after all, five pages of combinations I could try and then eliminate. I might not discover what the combination was, but at least I would know what it *wasn't*. I stood, uncrumpled the pages, and smoothed them until the numbers were once more legible. Wrinkled pages in hand, I headed down the companionway toward the chart room, determined not to be discouraged.

As I approached the door and reached for the knob, something peculiar happened. As though recoiling from my touch, the door slowly and silently swung inward without so much as a creak or a whisper.

I hesitated for a moment, and, taking my cue from the door itself, proceeded noiselessly, like a shadow. Halfway in, barely breathing, I stopped short, shocked at what I saw.

Without a sound I retreated into the corridor and

backed against the wall so as not to be seen. I turned my face to the right, affording me a view into the room while remaining somewhat out of sight.

Quaide squatted in front of the safe, his pants slipping just beneath the absurdly offensive crack of his backside. He inclined his ear toward the lock and spun the dial between chunky fingers, this way and that, this way and that. Then he abruptly stood, adjusted his trousers, and shrugged his wide, thickset shoulders. His fingers twitched, as though itching to do something.

Not wanting him to realize he'd been observed, I backed several yards down the narrow hallway, and as I did so the door eased itself shut. I took a deep breath, feigned a cough, then walked forward, shuffling my feet. The door opened just as I approached, and Quaide appeared, his face as slack and blank as usual, a rolled chart tucked beneath his arm.

"Cap'n needed a map," he mumbled. His face registered no expression at all, not a shred of guilt or discomfort revealed in his hooded eyes.

"Really?" I asked through thin lips, pressing the pages of numbers against my chest. Had I not observed him tinkering with the safe, I might have believed that retrieving the map had been his only mission.

If Quaide noticed the ice beneath my words he

didn't let on. "Yeah," he said. "A map." He ducked through the doorway and walked past.

I watched his hulking form retreat, his heavy boots thumping up the stairs and disappearing into the sunlight. I was left in the dim corridor, staring at the hatchway door swinging in his wake. What was he up to? A chill rippled through me as I called to mind his onshore meeting with the scar-faced scoundrel and the mysterious green-eyed man, their gesturing toward our ship, the memory of money changing hands, and Quaide's ongoing, thinly veiled contempt for me. None of it boded well.

A sound behind me made me jump.

"Good lord," Marni said, placing a hand on my arm. My shoulders dropped and I exhaled loudly. She took me in with a penetrating glance. "You're as tightly wound as a spring. After your triumphant display of steely composure up there in the rigging I'd have thought nothing could fluster you."

I turned to my friend and greatest supporter and took a deep breath. "Marni," I said quietly, "there's something I need to tell you. Up until now I wasn't sure it was important, but . . ."

"Go on then," she said. "But not here." She glanced about. "Let's go to my stateroom."

I followed her down the narrow hallway into her room. It was spacious compared to mine, and closely resembled our parlor back home. Fine oak paneling, detailed with carved, scrolled designs, a brass-and-crystal chandelier overhead. Oriental carpets in rich hues and furniture in the fabrics Mother so loved—brocades and velvets. Strange how Marni seemed as much a part of this space as Mother, the room embodying the strong, calming presence both of them evoked. Marni was right, as always. Having our conversation here in this sanctuary would be better.

Marni closed the door securely behind us. "Sit." She looked at me closely. "It's Quaide, isn't it?"

Judging from my raised eyebrows, she continued. "Surely one can't help but notice the resentment he hauls around like an anchor. I know everyone's been leery about him from the start, but we'll get to that. There's more, am I right?"

I nodded. Bit my lower lip.

"All right," she said kindly. "Out with it."

I took a deep breath. Stared into my lap. "Something happened back in port," I began. "In Boston." She watched me steadily with those translucent eyes of hers.

"Yes?"

"We should've told you, Georgie and me, but . . ."

"You're telling me now. Go on."

"When you and Addie and Walter went to the dry goods store, Georgie and I took a walk along the pier. Looking at ships and all the sights . . ."

"Nothing wrong in that."

"Yes, but . . . well . . ."

She inclined her head just slightly and leaned forward in the chair, eyeing me steadily. She nodded for me to continue.

I swallowed once. Twice. "Well, a man—this horrible man—grabbed me, well, there were two men—they snatched each of us, me and Georgie, tried to drag us off! To kidnap us! Force us into duty aboard their ship!"

The color drained from her face. She sat perfectly still except for the tightening of her fingers around the carved lion's heads on the wooden arms of her chair. Her very large silence pressed in on me. To fill the void, my words tumbled out. "Dirty scoundrels, they were—the one that got me had a scar—a big one . . . like this . . ." I drew my finger diagonally across my face, chin to opposite cheekbone. "A red scarf around his head. I kicked! Bit! He threw me to the ground! It was the . . ." I stopped abruptly before the word *cap'n* rolled off my tongue. I realized I didn't want to bring the captain into it. But it was too late now.

Expressionless, Marni coaxed, "It was the . . . ?"

"Captain," I said.

She sprang from the chair, her jade eyes turned to ice.

"No! No!" I corrected, waving my hands, trying to erase what I'd implied. "No, it was the cap'n who *rescued* us! Stepped in and pressed those vile characters to unhand Georgie and me!"

At this she eased into her seat, her back ramrod straight. Her steely gaze cut right through me. "Attempted kidnapping is a serious offense. He had a responsibility to report it to the authorities, regardless of whether or not they took it seriously." She placed her elbows on her knees, rested her chin in her hands. Disappeared inside herself for a few moments. She continued softly, almost as though she'd forgotten I was there, reasoning it out. "Although he might have speculated that an investigation would ensue—which could take weeks, delaying our departure. Or, perhaps he did report it, without involving you and Georgie." She sat up straight and dropped her hands. "I'll be asking him about this, you can be sure. But there's more, isn't there?"

I nodded, my head bobbing like a wobbling top. "Yes. The cap'n realized we couldn't—wouldn't . . ." I stuttered, shaking my head. "He realized we hadn't told you about it. And was kind not to . . ."

"Not to share information that he clearly knew I'd want to know?"

My heart sank. "It wasn't that, it was . . ."

"What else do I need to know?" she snapped.

"The other day—the day we set sail?"

"Yes . . ."

"Quaide said he had some last-minute business onshore."

"Um-hmmm . . ."

"Well, I was up on the poop deck with my spyglass, watching people up close along the pier. One looked like Mother—well, not really, but anyway, the spyglass suddenly moved on its own until it came to focus on Quaide! I saw him talking to the one who tried to kidnap me, the one with the scar—to him and another man, a man with these green eyes . . ." I realized his eyes were not unlike hers at the moment—steely and uncompromising. I went on, words tumbling like waves. "He—Quaide—pointed to our ship. Then, the green-eyed man gave them each a pile of money. I watched him count it into their hands! Then Quaide left them and rejoined us. And the ship—the one the pirate tried to drag us to? I've spotted it on the horizon, sailing a similar course."

Marni's lips were pulled taut. A fleeting, faraway look sailed across her face and she absently fingered the silver locket at her throat. "What else now? Put it all out there."

"Just now, before you saw me in the companion-way? I saw Quaide in the chart room fiddling with Father's safe! Kneeling there, trying to open it. The door to the chart room moved by itself, preventing me from being seen! He didn't notice me—this I'm sure of." I was nearly breathless, my heart racing at the breadth of my confession. I waited.

"Well, let's look at this one piece at a time. In the first place, you didn't tell me of the kidnapping because you thought it was somehow your fault?"

"It *was* my fault, should have been more care-ful. I didn't want to let you down. I—"

"It wasn't your fault. Lucy?"

I looked up.

"It wasn't your fault. This sort of thing has occurred as long as there have been ships to sail, work to be done, money to be made. You were not responsible. But keeping it a secret was a mistake. Then, I suppose, as often happens, one omission leads to another."

I nodded. "Yes . . ."

"Unfortunately, the second omission—this busi-ness onshore between Quaide and these men—is concerning in an altogether different way. But it confirms my instincts about the man."

"But if you felt that way about Quaide, why did we hire him?"

Marni sat forward. She stared over my head at some distant spot, real or imagined, and her eyes narrowed. "I had a strong feeling about him," she said. "I disliked him, as I know you do. But he felt integral to some bigger plan. My instinct told me he would be important to this quest in some way. And I've learned, through the years, to listen to my instincts."

"But what do we *do?*"

She sat back, thoughtful.

"First, I intend to have a few words with the captain. He must know that he exercised poor, though well-intentioned, judgment in helping to keep your secret. Secondly, he must know our concerns about Quaide. Third, we must have a family meeting—everyone must be vigilant, cautious. And," she added pointedly, "forthcoming in all things."

"I'm sorry, Marni," I began.

She silenced me with a gentle raised hand. "We understand each other, that's what's important."

She stood, and seemed taller to me than usual. She flashed a smile. "There is good news in all of this! It seems the magic that transformed this ship is once again your ally! Come along with me to the helm," she said. "You can take over the wheel for a bit, while the captain and I have a little talk."

8

At the helm—the knobs of the ship's wheel secure in my fisted hands, the wind in my hair—it was relatively easy to put aside my worries, at least for the moment. Grady hollered out directions (perhaps from the chart Quaide had retrieved?): "Sou' by sou'east. . . . Keep 'er close t' the wind!" This I was able to do almost on instinct. That we were far from rocky coastlines, and there were no other ships in sight, no doubt lent to my air of confidence—we were, by all estimations, about a week from the Azore Islands. Georgie eyed me jealously from his bell platform, sounding the next half-hour mark. "No fair!" he muttered, clanging the bell with unnecessary vigor, the rest of his complaint lost to the crash of the waves.

It wasn't long before Marni and Captain Adams strolled back, side by side, their heads inclined. I glanced their way and then out to sea, suddenly uncomfortable, anxious to have the awkward exchange that was sure to take place over with.

"You make a good helmswoman, Miss Lucy," he said with a smile. "Must be in your blood!" I stepped aside, avoiding his eyes, and he took back the wheel. "It's always good to have the air cleared, wouldn't you agree? A squall, while challenging, usually yields blue skies in its wake." I could detect nothing in his tone but affection.

"Yes, Cap'n," I said. Like Marni, the cap'n had a knack for moving through difficult places with ease and grace. What more could we want when we hit the inevitable storms at sea?

The cap'n went on, not at all defensively. "And to allay any concerns about my judgment, you deserve to know that I did alert the authorities in regard to that miserable character who attempted to abduct you. As a father myself . . ." He paused, as though he had misspoken. "Well . . . suffice it to say I am always concerned for the welfare of children."

"You have children?" I asked, my curiosity piqued.

A shadow crossed the cap'n's face. "I did."

Marni gently touched my arm, a cue for me not to press. The subtle gesture didn't escape the cap'n's eye. "It's all right, Miss Marni." He turned to me. "I had a daughter, Imogene. A feisty little sprig of a girl." His eyes filled with a flash of delight at the mention of her. And then they changed. "Influenza," he said, quietly, "took her from me, and her mother as well."

My heart wrenched, understanding what it meant to lose those you care about the most. At least for me there was Aunt Pru. "Oh, I'm so sorry, Cap'n!"

"Yes, of course you are. Thank you, Miss Lucy. Now, what do you say we get back to the business of sailing this ship?"

I met his eyes, and, in light of all of this, wondered if Marni had shared our concerns about Quaide. As if my worry had conjured him up, the hulking figure appeared. He moved toward Georgie, who sat on his platform, arms crossed, chin resting on his knees, his envy toward me at the helm evidenced by his curled, petulant lower lip and creased brow. Quaide squatted beside him, nudged Georgie with his elbow, and gestured toward the foremast.

"Cap'n," Quaide called. "Might we out the stun's'l? Show the kid what kinda speed she got?"

Cap'n nodded good-naturedly. "Out studding sails!" he shouted. Quaide poked Georgie with a thick finger. "Wanna be a sailor, don'tcha? Come on. Stick with me. Ya can help me run out the booms." Georgie scrambled up and followed him. If he'd had a tail, like Pugsley, he'd be wagging it.

"Good for the little one to learn," said the cap'n. "Nice to see Quaide take him under wing."

"We'll see," Marni said quietly. She and I exchanged a glance that told me she hadn't yet brought Quaide and his questionable motives to the captain's attention. With a nod to the cap'n, and a hand on my shoulder, she led me away. "No better time than now for a family meeting," she said. "Go round up Walter and Addie. In the stateroom." She went her way and I mine, a sense of urgency suddenly propelling us both.

Once gathered, Marni waved Rasjohnny in, a tray of coffee and sweet biscuits in his hands. "Der ya go, missus," he said, and was gone, closing the door snugly behind him. The four of us sat around the parlor table, stirring and sipping. It felt very grown-up to be part of this. Until I thought about what had to be said. How they would all hear about the attempted kidnapping. KID-napping, I thought miserably. I glanced over my cup at Walter, who was dunking his biscuit. He lifted the java-saturated treat, tipped his head, and opened his mouth just as the biscuit-turned-to-mush plopped in his lap. I laughed and, for a moment, felt better.

Just then Addie reached out and patted my hand. "I've been missin' ya, Lucy, I 'ave," she said. "Used to be we spent more time t'gether. Now, all of a sudden, you're off on yer own, doin' what needs doin,' as though you been doin' it all yer life! The cap'n'd be proud." She blushed. "I meant yer father, of course, Cap'n Simmons!"

I bit my lip. She'd feel differently when she heard what had almost happened. Marni jumped in. "We don't have much time, what with all our respective responsibilities, so let me get right to it."

I took a deep breath.

"Quaide," she said. "There is reason to believe we shouldn't trust him. Lucy saw him involved in a dubious transaction involving some riff-raff onshore. Money changed hands." She looked from Walter to Addie, both listening with rapt attention. "This alone might not suggest anything other than the dealings of a rough-and-tumble seaman. But there's more. Lucy, tell them what you saw in the chart room."

I swallowed, felt all eyes on me. "He didn't see

me—I was in the passageway and the door to the chart room opened of its own accord—silently. Of course, I looked inside. Quaide was in there, trying to open the safe."

"I've seen the safe," Walter said. "Was going to ask about it."

"It was Father's safe, and it's locked. Besides money or valuables, it could hold clues to Aunt Pru's whereabouts. I don't know the combination. But I feel I can figure it out. I have to!"

Marni nodded. "Yes. It's important, I believe, to discover what secrets or treasures the safe might hold. Quaide, I'm sure, is more interested in monetary gain."

"I didn't trust him from the start," Walter said. "It's just that he looked like he could carry his weight. And he is a good sailor."

Addie leaned forward, wagging her finger. "Has a bit o' crudeness to 'im, he does."

"A *bit*?" Walter said, and I stifled a laugh.

Addie gathered herself up and looked at Walter defensively. "I was bein' polite."

"Crude, he is," Marni continued, "but crude is not the real problem. Trustworthiness is the issue. All I'm saying is, be watchful. For such a large fellow he has the ability to be stealthy. Keep him in your sights. Mind his movements. And if you see anything that concerns you—even a little—share it. Between the four of us . . . are we agreed?"

We offered our unanimous assent, stood, and prepared to leave. Addie reached out for me. "We'll need t' attend to daily lessons," she said. "Book learnin' is important fer ye, along with Annie and Master Georgie."

I snapped, "I'm not a child!" Marni raised an eyebrow, and I instantly regretted my tone. Addie looked stricken. Walter tried, unsuccessfully, not to gloat.

"But yes, Addie," I amended, softening my voice. "I'd love to read with you. And Annie and Georgie."

"'Twould do ye all good!" Addie said, a trace of resentment in her voice. "'Twouldn't hurt ye, Walter, neither!"

"No it wouldn't," I agreed. "Let's include him!"

"All right then," Marni said, rising from her chair, gathering the tray of coffee. "Let's get on with it!" As she led the way out of the stateroom, followed by Addie, Walter took my arm and pulled me back.

He whispered, "You said the door opened of its own accord." His dark eyes shone. "The magic—I was thinking that maybe we'd left it back in Maine. Do you think . . . ?"

"Yes," I said. "And that's not all. When I spied Quaide onshore with Father's spyglass . . . it moved, as though guided by an iron hand, until it focused on what I needed to see. . . ."

"I could have guessed," he said. "Because when I was on watch, I saw something out there on the sea . . ."

We inched closer together. "Yes—a ship? On the horizon . . ."

"Almost flying above the waves," he said, finishing my sentence, "following at a distance." I could feel his breath on my face. "It was as though it was . . . I don't know . . . stalking us. . . ."

"And the glittering cloud," I continued, the words tumbling. "I wasn't sure—I thought it might have just been a rainbow in the mist, but—"

"Yes! Yes—it surrounded the vessel!"

I placed my hand on his forearm. "When I was up at the top of the mast . . ." I was about to tell him of Father's voice instructing me when I dangled from the royal yard. He leaned closer. We were nearly nose to nose. My heart raced. "What?" he asked, his eyes alive with excitement, and something else.

But Father's words, I realized, I wanted to keep for myself. That, and the discomfort I felt boasting of Father, strong and benevolent even in death, compared to the brute of a man who called Walter his son.

"What else?" he persisted.

I backed away. Removed my hand from his arm. "Nothing," I said.

"No, there's more—I can see it in your eyes."

I shook my head. Looked down. Felt him pull away. In a moment everything had changed.

The bell sounded. "Time for my watch," he mumbled.

"Walter," I called after him. "Walter!"

But he was already gone.

9

It had been thirteen days a-sail, with no land in sight. I found myself always looking to the east, in anticipation of our first landmark, but the Azore Islands were still days, maybe even a week, away. I wandered below, into the stateroom, the familiarity engulfing me in a sense of the past. There, Mother's needlepoint pillow, here, Father's oak rocker. I sat in the ornate chair and pushed back with my feet. It creaked in the accustomed manner, lulling me in rhythm with the gentle swaying of the ship. I closed my eyes and could almost believe I was back home in Maine, that any moment Father would enter, our copy of *Treasure Island* in hand for our next installment. Roaming the room, my gaze settled on a small wooden chest in the corner that I hadn't noticed before. The ship creaked as it pitched, sending the chest sliding across the varnished floor, stopping inches from my feet. It was as though the vessel had offered me a gift. "Thank you," I whispered, staring at the wooden box. The letters **ES** were stenciled on the front in black—Father's initials! Was it his ditty box from long-ago days at sea?

I went to the chest, knelt before it, and ran my hand over the rough, dark green–painted surface. A dull brass latch on the front may have once held a lock but now hung unencumbered. The hinged lid squeaked as I slowly lifted it open.

I removed the contents, one item at a time. Expecting it to be filled with the practicalities of a seaman, I was surprised to discover several pieces of ivory—whalebone or, perhaps, walrus tusk, decorated with designs and scenes of the sea. Tucked alongside was a small suede sack holding a number of crude sailing needles and pointed etching tools—a scrimshaw set for carving and decorating whalebone! Next, I pulled out a leather satchel folded in thirds. I untied the rawhide cord and opened it to find a collection of knives, chisels, and gouging tools perfect for carving. Then, a pen-and-ink set—miniature bottles of black, indigo, and red inks, and a graceful quill with a variety of nibs.

A sound outside made me jump. "What are you doing, Lucy?"

Annie stood in the doorway. Ida butted past her, trotted over, and began nibbling the suede sack I'd set on the floor. "Ida! Bad nanny!" Annie cried, running in. "Ooh!" she said, stopping short, forgetting all about Ida. "What's that?" She pointed into the chest, and pulled out an octagon-shaped frame with the beginnings of a mosaic of delicate pastel seashells inside.

"A sailor's valentine," I mused, wondering if Father had begun crafting it for my mother during lonely nights at sea.

"And this?" Annie marveled, her blue eyes open wide. In one hand she held a rectangular wooden box with an inlaid design of mother-of-pearl. "A jewelry box!" she exclaimed, holding it out in front of her. "Or . . . or . . . a pirate treasure!" A dark thought crossed my mind. It didn't look like a jewelry box, and was certainly too small to be a treasure chest—it looked like . . . a miniature coffin. I pushed the thought from my mind. "Open it," I said.

The two of us, heads together, strained for a

peek. "What in the world?" I mumbled. The box held a deck of playing cards, stacked in two piles. I took one and held it up. The back of the card had been decorated in an incredibly intricate design of scrolls and swirls, a web of fine curlicue lines that surrounded a tiny figure of a seaman here, a whale there. It had been done by hand, I was sure.

"Turn it over!" Annie commanded excitedly.

I flipped the card to the face side, revealing the queen of spades.

"Oh my!" Annie gasped.

What a queen she was. A black three-cornered hat sat on her head, long black curls tumbling beneath it. Thick golden hoops dangled from her ears. She wore a white ruffled blouse tied at her waist, the pointy collar unbuttoned to an indecent depth, revealing a hint of her abundant breasts. A short, tight-fitting scarlet vest hugged her torso. She smiled wickedly, chin resting on a fisted hand. A large blue ring graced her index finger and a column of jeweled bracelets circled her wrist. Her other arm, bent at the elbow, pointed up, a flint-lock pistol in her grasp. Her green, narrowed eyes seemed to be watching us mockingly, as if she knew something we didn't.

Annie and I quickly removed the entire col-lection of cards, spreading them across the floor, fighting off Ida, who seemed to find them appetizing. We separated and studied the face cards—a collection of characters, the likes of which we had never seen. The kings and jacks—some were refined and genteel, others wild and whiskered. The same with the queens, although none as striking as the queen of spades. Each character had initials somewhere on the card, the queen of spades labeled **MML**. The king of diamonds stood out as well—a nobleman dressed in finery—a white ruffled shirt topped with a royal-blue vest and a golden waistcoat, the lapels and cuffs decorated with fancy trimmings. His expression, however, was anything but gentlemanly. He had the look of a sly fox, his smile a snarling curl of the lip. One fisted hand held at his heart overflowed with strands of pearls and jewels. Columns of gold and silver coins formed small towers before him. I gasped as I saw the letters beneath the portrait—**ES**. Father's initials. I shook my head. What foolishness! As though Father could have anything to do with the likes of this character. A coincidence was all.

As I laid the queen of spades and king of diamonds side by side, I felt a jolt of static electricity in my fingers, and yanked my hand back. The two cards began to quiver and shimmy. Annie and I exchanged a glance, her eyes round as saucers.

Then the queen of spades flew into the air, as though flipped by an invisible hand, hovered for a moment before landing with a force that blew the king of diamonds, facedown, several inches away.

Annie looked up at me. "Magic cards," she whispered. "Can I have them?" I raised an eyebrow. Clearly, they were not mere playthings. But the longing on her face tugged at me.

"We can keep them," I said. "You and I together. These are no ordinary cards. I'm sure they hold some secrets. We'll hide them in our cabin, where we'll take extra-special care of them." She nodded gravely.

"We can't lose a single one of them, or bend them, or get them wet." I glanced at Ida. "Or let the goat eat them!"

"I won't, Lucy, I promise!"

"All right." I reached for the queen of spades hesitantly, bracing for another electrical jolt, but there was none. "I'll gather these up and put them back in the box in two piles. I think it's important we keep the queen of spades and the king of diamonds in separate stacks." As if in assent the queen of spades somersaulted into my hand, and the king of diamonds blew an inch or two in the opposite direction. I sorted the remaining cards into two piles and began tucking them into the wooden box.

I placed the king of diamonds at the bottom right, the queen of spades top left, and closed the lid. Annie grabbed the box and hugged it to her chest.

"Remember what I said," I warned, as she skipped from the room, Ida at her heels.

I looked at the variety of amusements the ditty box had yielded—something for each of us, I thought. Perhaps Georgie could try his hand at carving—I bet Javan could help him. For me, the pen-and-ink set. Walter might like the scrimshaw. I blushed as another thought crossed my mind. Maybe he would complete the sailor's valentine for someone special. Embarrassed by my own imagination, I picked up the octagonal frame and returned it to the box.

There was something else at the bottom of the chest that I'd missed. I pushed the valentine aside and pulled out a large book, its cardboard binding deteriorating, the edges of its yellowed pages flaking in my hands. The title read: *Chanteys and Songs of the Sea*, and the cover depicted a group of sailors aboard a ship, their mouths all open *O*s as though singing a rousing chorus together.

With a musty *poof!* the cover flew open and the pages ruffled and fanned forward and back, faster and faster. A tingling energy emanated from the steady breeze of the aged pages, and then a glittering, colorful cloud wafted from the fragile volume. It swirled around me like a refreshing mist from the sea. A faint, hollow sound accompanied the mist, which crescendoed until the pages slowed their ruffling and settled. The sparkling vapor dissipated. I rubbed my eyes and blinked at the open book. Crude blotted notes danced across ribbons of handwritten staves that striped the page. If the song had a title, it was gone, the top of the leaf having disintegrated. The reedy sound increased in volume and was joined by another—the second part of the duet pouring from the flute in my pocket! I reached for it, but the slim instrument was already weaving its way from between the folds of cloth, and in an instant was bobbing in the air before me. The melodies of two flutes, one visible, the other invisible, crisscrossed and intertwined, until they met on a common pitch and became a single melodic line. Tone by tone, the corresponding notes on the page blinked in a rainbow of colors, as each sounded in turn. The resulting tune I knew as well as my own name. It was the song Father had taught me, the one in which the words had been all but forgotten, except for the chorus—*a la dee dah dah . . . a la dee dah dee!* I realized that, for the first time, I was seeing the notes I'd learned by rote, illuminated, one by one.

Suddenly the melody stopped. The ship changed direction, tacking unexpectedly to starboard. My flute dropped to the floor and rolled. On hands and knees I scrambled for it, now careening beneath the rocker. I reached, and then, without warning, we tacked to portside, throwing me off balance. Three times, in short succession, the *Lucy P. Simmons* was nearly put about, listing one way, then the other.

"All hands! All hands!"

The ship's bell clanged wildly. An army of frantic footsteps pounded the deck above me.

I scrambled to my feet, flew through the doorway, along the companionway, and up the steps. The air outside was as charged as the sky before a thunderstorm. A heavy mist swirled like a phantom over the water, its tendrils of cool vapor wafting across the deck and raising gooseflesh on my arms and up my spine.

The cap'n was at the helm, straining at the wheel, our ship tilting dramatically as it cut into the wind across her own wake. There was a schooner close aboard, windward on the larboard bow, under full sail, on a collision course with our ship! I squinted through the fog. Could it be the same ship I'd seen aloft? The sea began to roil, whitecaps crashing, sheets of water obscuring my view. There was no time for a second thought. I joined Walter, the Reds, Tonio, and Quaide, frantically working the sails. Pugsley circled about, yipping and growling. Grady hung by one arm in the crow's nest, leaning out over the sea, his spyglass extended. He shouted something down to Coleman, and Coleman and Irish ran to secure the lines. Again we abruptly tacked; the *Lucy P. Simmons* put about in the opposite direction. "Hold your course!" Quaide yelled, his fist in the air. "Pitch, pitch! To hell your soul! The more you pitch, the less you'll roll!" Georgie's voice mimicked Quaide's: "Pitch, pitch! To hell your soul! The more you pitch, the less you'll roll!"

But still, unbelievably, the schooner was once more approaching on opposite tacks, her bow rolling over the waves, her bowsprit cutting through the mist, aiming toward us like a harpoon bearing down on a whale. Staring at the approaching ship, I dashed toward the nearest ratline and began to climb.

Higher, higher, the view of the advancing vessel clearer, brighter, the voices and turmoil below dim and distant. The schooner shimmered against the sky. Flew above the waves. I blinked, then fixed my line of vision, toward the radiant ship—the very same ship Walter and I'd seen before. I was barely aware of scooting out across the spar to the end of the yardarm, or of the churning ocean beneath me. A high-pitched hum emanated from the schooner, and drew me farther and farther out. My ears rang, blotting out the cries of Marni and Addie, Walter, and the cap'n, the Reds and Irish too. The hum increased, this chorus of other voices, a babble of words. I strained to distinguish one from the other, hearing only enough to make me want more.

Then, a glimpse of motion on board the schooner, phantom shadows of figures on deck, graceful movements, dancing to the thrum of the ghostly chorus.

Our ship tipped again and I was suddenly airborne, sailing through clouds, soaring over water, a seabird on the wing.

A kaleidoscope of sails, sky, sea. A flash of deck and bow.

I hit the water hard. It swallowed me whole. Sucked me down until all was still.

10

I rose through the water, my hair streaming about me like seaweed. Floated upward toward the light—weightless, buoyant. An angel of the sea.

I had only a vague sense of being hauled from the ocean. I saw nothing, and heard only the muffled gurgling of trapped air and moving water. Curiously, I was not afraid. No thrashing or flailing about. No desperate thoughts of rescue or escape. Instead, I let myself be handled by unseen arms, if they were arms at all. Perhaps this was what it meant to be dead.

And then I was standing, but could not feel solid

ground beneath my feet. Wet, but not dripping. Alive, but not breathing. Seeing through closed eyes. I was there, but not there, in a stateroom of a ship, a chamber with low ceilings and dim light. An invisible barrier kept me from the others gathered there, a field of energy like glass, me on one side, the rest on the other.

They sat around what appeared to be a long low chest, filmy figures that flickered and reflected light. In fact, luminous air seemed to move right through them, their shimmering silhouettes more pronounced than their individual features. The entire scene wavered before me like heat rising off a roadway in the dog days of summer. Some of the figures were strangely familiar in an unnameable way. They were engaged in a card game, seven of them in all. The flutter and snap of shuffling cards, the hum of voices, and the electricity of anticipation bounced against me. The more I concentrated, the more their features took shape, at least those closest to me, but only in a transparent, fleeting fashion. Likewise, I got a diffuse glimpse of their clothing, and their manner of movement. Through the sheer force of my resolve their faces came into focus, as I watched them in my mind's eye.

I gasped, my lungs straining, as recognition hit me like a bolt of lightning.

Father held the deck of cards, staring at me intently. He shuffled them, flipped the pile back in a rush, transferred the deck to one hand, and strummed the edges of the stack with the other. The sound was hypnotizing. *Pay attention, Lucy,* his silent voice commanded. Over and over he thumbed the edge of the deck.

Stop shuffling and deal! This coming from the figure to Father's left—an impression of his thin face and black beady eyes flashed for an instant— Uncle Victor! *There's no rush, not now, except for Lucy to learn what she must.* It was my mother, seated to Father's right, her delicate hand reaching toward me. Affection curved the edges of her lips. Everything inside me became soft with longing. I moved, in slow motion, as through a sea of gel, but no matter how I tried to project myself forward, I remained a stone's throw from her. *It's all in the cards, dear one,* she whispered.

A man across from Father waved a hand toward me. *She's our last hope, this one—she and my Pru.* He patted my mother's hand. *But I have confidence in her.*

My Pru . . . he was my grandfather—Father's father! I knew this without ever having seen the man. And he saw my aunt and me together—his last hope! To his left was my aunt Margaret, a card grasped protectively in her pudgy hands, her eyes darting about nervously.

Two other figures, the faintest of all, sat opposite each other at the far end of the group. They leaned across the surface of the dark chest, staring at each other, eye to eye, with an intensity that drew them together and, at the same time, repelled them, a black energy between them sizzling like the sky before a thunderstorm. *You played your cards,* the woman hissed, *but you lost the game! Just look around!* She gestured among the players.

The man chuckled. *It isn't over till it's over!*

Abruptly she stood, toppling her chair, and addressed her adversary again. *Is she your next wager? She's in the game now, like it or not. And YOU!* She whirled around and pointed at me, her glittering eyes narrowed. As though directed by her gaze, a frigid current of air engulfed me. I gasped, flailing my arms, a suffocating pressure bearing down on my chest. *You'd better learn the rules of the game! Not a word of this to any of your mates! That would be cheating. Do I make myself clear?*

Yes! I silently screamed, teeth chattering. Yes! The cold receded, leaving me shuddering convulsively.

Glad we understand each other! She turned back toward her opponent. *And cheaters never prosper, isn't that right?* She took hold of the edge of the chest and threw open what I now realized was a lid, sending the cards and coins sliding to the ground. The cover of the chest was inlaid with mother-of-pearl, its shape now unmistakable. It wasn't a chest, but a coffin—its miniature replica back on board our ship, holding the cards Annie and I had discovered!

The man across from the threatening woman grinned slyly and slammed the top shut with one hand, his cards still pressed securely against his vest. *You're bluffing. I'm not folding! I'll bet my money on the girl and play my hand to the end!*

In that moment, I recognized them—she, the queen of spades. He, the king of diamonds!

With that realization, I was violently lifted and thrown from the room, engulfed again in water and waves. I jerked to the surface, coughing. Spewing. Lungs bursting. Someone grabbed my wrist, wrenched it behind my back. Twisting, I was subdued by an iron arm clamped across my chest. Steely fingers locked in the hollow beneath my arm. I thrashed. Smacked the water with my free hand, desperately trying to regain control.

Again, underwater, until I broke the surface once more, gasping and gulping. The blinding blue sky assaulted my eyes.

The bow of a dinghy bobbed closer and closer, amidst an array of floating objects—a carpenter's bench, a life buoy, a wooden shelf. A hand reached over the side of the rescue boat, latched on to my arm, and yanked. My chest thumped against the hull, and the viselike arms around me pushed and prodded until I was thrust over the edge of the small vessel, flopping about like a fish on a hook. Walter's face came into view above mine, his features a tug of war between panic and relief. Then a splash, the boat dipped, and I heard someone climbing over the side. One narrow, bare, dripping foot, then another flapped beside me.

I struggled to sit, Walter's arms pushing me back, but still I managed to pull myself up. "Easy does it, Lucy," he said. "Careful!"

Marni knelt beside me, her silver hair slick to her head, chest heaving, her face knotted in concern. Her dripping arms trembled from exertion. The captain, along with a collection of faces, peered down over the starboard rail of our ship, her prow looming over us. I looked up at the two carrottops, Tonio's shining bald dome, Irish's head of black curls, and Coleman's faded features. Rasjohnny waved his arms wildly. I heard Addie's voice, high-pitched and thick with emotion. "T'ank the Lord, she's alive, she is!"

"She's got herself sittin' up pretty," Rasjohnny called. "Yessiree, she do. Miss Annie, ya can stop yer bawlin' now! Pugsley, stop yer howlin'! Everything gonna be okay!"

"Lower the rope!" the cap'n hollered. "Be quick about it!"

Rasjohnny heaved a rope ladder over the side. It thwacked against the boat's wooden timbers as it unfurled and hit the water several yards from where we were. Walter grabbed the oars and rowed toward it. Under Quaide's direction, Georgie threw a line attached to a makeshift harness crafted from a thick leather belt. "Just in case," Quaide shouted. I could hear the sneer in his voice. "Strap it around so if ya don't make it up ya won't fall in again."

"I'm right here!" Walter shouted. "I won't let either of them fall!" He looked intently at me. "You girls ready?"

"Hey, kid," Quaide called to Walter. "Collect all the floatin' stuff we threw overboard fer nothin'. No sense lettin' it all wash away."

I looked at Marni, still catching her breath. She closed her eyes and nodded.

"Marni . . ." I began, suddenly overwhelmed with emotion. This was the second time she'd pulled me from the sea half dead—the first back in Maine, when Mother and Father had drowned. And now again. I reached toward her. "Thank you."

She opened her eyes and fingered the locket at her throat. "I couldn't lose another one," she said, her voice husky and spent. "Let's get you back aboard."

Walter grabbed the belt and strapped it around my waist. "Can you climb?" he asked.

My arms and legs felt like jelly. "I think so."

I grasped the ladder several rungs up and planted my foot on the bottom one.

"Here she comes!" Addie yelled. "Be careful, child! Oh sweet Jesus, I can't bear to look!"

I climbed slowly, muscles quivering. Kept my eyes peeled straight ahead so as not to think about the distance between the deck and the ocean. Walter was right behind me. "Atta girl, Luce. Yup. One more. That's the way!"

After what seemed like an eternity I chanced an upward glance. The cap'n leaned over, arms outstretched, Coleman and Irish on either side of him. "Take my hands!" Cap'n shouted. I reached up and he clasped my forearms with strong, sure fingers. Up, up, they hoisted me, Quaide cranking the harness line over a squeaky winch. In one last burst my legs dropped over the side to the cheers of our crew. The Reds stood back awkwardly, wringing their hands, tentative smiles on their matching pale faces. Tonio gave a sharp salute with two fingers. His thick black mustache twitched. Coleman sighed heavily, raking his fingers through his tuft of goose-down hair.

Then, Addie was beside me, her fingers running over my cheeks like hungry tentacles. She swept me into her arms and hugged me with a force that threatened to cut off what breath I had left. Pugsley leaped in the air over and over, panting and wagging his curlicue tail. Annie wrapped her arms around my legs and squeezed, and Ida bleated and butted me with her head. Georgie stared at me, his eyes giant *O*s. "You was nearly drowned!" he said, incredulous. "What'd you go and jump for, anyway? I saw you *jump*!"

"Georgie!" Addie admonished. "Don't be speakin' such nonsense! Course she didn't jump! Why would she do that, I ask ye?"

Quaide smirked. Grady shrunk back, peering at me through narrowed eyes, rubbing thumbs and index fingers together. "And where's the schooner?" he asked, his head bobbing. "Anybody care to answer that? A specter ship, I tell ye, perhaps the *Flying Dutchman* itself! Disappeared as soon as the little missy here took the plunge. Lured, she was, by a siren's song or such. It ain't right. Ain't normal." He clamped his mouth shut when Marni pulled herself over the side, the cap'n surrounding her with a blanket. Javan pressed steaming mugs of coffee into our hands, as Walter climbed over, took up the ladder, and prepared to raise the lifeboat. "It ain't right," Grady repeated. I looked out to sea. Grady was right. There was no sign of the phantom vessel. It had vanished.

"No means of identifying the ship," the cap'n mused. "No name. No markings. Spotted her at a distance a few times. How she managed to move out of range this quickly is a mystery to me." The men stared at the horizon, Irish scratching his head, the Reds frowning, Tonio pursing and unpursing his lips.

"Enter it into the log, Coleman," the cap'n said. "The rest of you—be watchful. On the ready!" As the crew dispersed he stared out across the water, concern knitting his brow.

"Come," Marni said, placing an arm around me. "We both need to get out of these wet clothes. Rest. Then we can talk about what happened out there."

She studied me with her deep green eyes. Had she gotten a glimpse of them? Or was it that sixth sense of hers that always seemed to guide her where she was needed most? Arm in arm we headed below, me to my cabin and Marni to hers.

I stripped off my wet clothing and dried myself

with a towel sheet. Put on my softest, oldest shirt and cozy frayed trousers and fell into the hammock. It rocked back and forth, back and forth. I stared at the ceiling. My mother's face appeared in my mind's eye, and I thrilled at the memory of it. And Father. Victor and Margaret. I shuddered at the thought of them. All of them. All of the Simmonses who'd died at sea. And the other two—the queen and king. I shivered, recalling her words: *Your next wager? You want her to join the game?* And the king: *I'll play my hand till the end!*

The curse. They were all talking about the curse.

She's our last hope, this one—she and my Pru. That's what my grandfather had said. And the queen of spades—*Not a word of this to any of your mates! That would be cheating.* Pru, I thought, how I wish you were here with me! What would you make out of all of this?

A gripping chill raised gooseflesh along my arms. I felt cold down to my bones. Shut my eyes, but all I could hear was the sound of phantom cards shuffling, snapping. And Mother's words: *It's all in the cards, dear one.*

11

We sat huddled together in Marni's state-room, Walter, Addie, Marni, and me, the ditty box of amusements there where I'd left it. Together we connected the pieces of the events that had unfolded.

Grady, on watch, had spotted the schooner first. He'd sounded the call and the cap'n had adjusted our course accordingly. No cause for concern just yet, except, according to all accounts, the peculiar ship continued to bear down on us, no matter which way we tacked. And that wasn't all—the way the advancing ship seemed to shimmer and glow, almost above the waves, skimming the surface like a seabird.

"Never have I witnessed the likes of it," Addie said, shaking her head. "Save for, of course, back in Maine, with the passin' o' the mansion into the sea. 'Twas of the same source, these goings-on. Indeed it 'twas!"

"And then, there we were," Walter said, "struggling with the sails, doing all we could to turn her around, and I see you, Lucy, sailing through the air. Hit the water and disappear."

I felt my face color.

"What happened, child?" Addie asked. "What were ye doin' up there in them ropes durin' such an emergency?"

Marni's emerald eyes studied me closely.

"I'm . . . not sure," I mumbled. "I . . . didn't think at all, really. . . . I saw the ship and then . . . I was scaling the ratline. I didn't intend to climb out to the yardarm, but . . ."

"It was like Grady said, wasn't it?" Walter asked quietly. "That was no ordinary ship. Something about it lured you."

"I had no choice." As the words left my mouth, I felt the weighty truth of them. Terrifying that I could be drawn into danger against my will. And yet, I'd seen Mother. Father. Felt their love . . .

Addie wrung her hands, her eyes wide, as though reliving the scene again. "In the mayhem of it all, Miss Marni—they tried to hold 'er back, they did, but she dove right over the side—Georgie and Javan and me heavin' anything overboard that'd float, in hopes of ye grabbin' hold! Coleman, quiet ghost that he is—never saw 'im move so fast as when he pitched the life ring o'er the side. Walter lowerin' the dinghy with breakneck speed. Thought we'd lose ye both! But in a flash, between the life ring and the wooden bench, there she was—Miss Marni—haulin' ye up out o' the deep!"

Marni, a far-off look in her eyes, ran her hand along the ornate wooden trim that framed the inside of the cabin. "That ship—the specter ship—I have the feeling it shares the same source of power as our own vessel—that they're connected in some way. If that's the case, I suppose it shouldn't be surprising that we're drawn together—like sister ships pulled by a force we can't understand. The question is, why? She must hold some secrets necessary for our quest."

I was amazed, as always, by Marni's instincts. Before I could respond, I spied the shadow of two large feet outside the stateroom door. Marni raised an eyebrow, almost imperceptibly. Bolted and shoved open the door.

Quaide, hunched forward, straightened up, turned, and walked on, but it was clear he'd been eavesdropping.

"Stop right there!" Marni commanded. "What do you think you're doing, skulking about?"

He shrugged, arms hanging by his sides, fingers opening and closing. He chewed the inside of one cheek, distorting his face. "Wasn't doin' nothin'," he mumbled. "Just stopped to . . . buckle me shoe." An insolent smirk inched across his mouth and pulled his face back to normal.

Marni stepped up, her face within inches of his. Her voice dropped to just above a whisper. "I'm watching you, Quaide. We're all watching you. And—trust me—I'll be having a word with the cap'n."

He shrugged again, shoulders creeping up his thick neck. His tongue swept across his fleshy lips, circling top to bottom. "Nothin' you could say to the cap'n that'd be concernin' me." He hulked toward the companionway, letting the door to the stairway bang behind him.

"Everybody, keep an eye on him," Marni said. "I notice he's taken Georgie under wing—having him help run out the booms, the studding sails. Feigning an interest that doesn't feel genuine to me. We need to watch that closely. The boy's

impressionable. Quaide's motives are seldom anything but self-serving."

"Don't worry about Georgie," Walter said. "I'll
be sure he's on the straight and narrow. It's my job,
after all."

"Good," Marni replied. "Let's try and keep that
specter ship in our sights. Hopefully, it will prove to
be a force for good. . . ." She glanced at me, her eyes
a question. I nodded. I hoped so too. Marni stood
up. "I think we've discussed all of this enough for
now. Lucy here's been through a lot."

I smiled at her faintly with my eyes. How was
she always able to read my heart? She and I both
knew there was more. But I thought of the queen
of spades's warning: *Not a word of this to any of your
mates! That would be cheating.* How I longed to tell
Marni what I'd seen, but I bit my tongue. "I am a
little tired," I said.

"You sure you're all right?" Walter asked.

I nodded. We walked together to the door,
Walter and I behind the others. "Oh, wait," I said,
tugging his sleeve. "Look what I found!"

I pulled out the ditty box and spread the contents on the floor, gladly putting off returning to
my cabin. Once I was alone I'd be forced to think
about what had happened. I hoped he didn't notice
the tremble that shook me as I picked up the book

of chanteys and the pen-and-ink set and gestured toward the rest. "Amusements for days at sea . . . take what you'd like and give the rest to Georgie and Javan."

"Swell!" he said. He knelt, fingered the leather satchel of carving tools, turned the scrimshaw over in his hands. "Something to capture Georgie's attention besides Quaide."

"You can have all of it. Annie and I already got what we wanted." The thought of taking the cards back from Annie crossed my mind, but that would make her want them all the more. I thought of the queen of spades. King of diamonds. I'd need to stress to Annie, again, the importance of handling them with care. She was a child, after all, and could lose them, or let that fool goat eat them. Suddenly I felt an urgency to get to my cabin, to inspect the cards again.

I scooped everything back into the chest. "Keep the box as well," I said, placing it in his hands. Before he could say another word I hustled him through the door, pushed past him, and turned in the direction of my cabin. I felt his eyes following me and stopped. "I don't think I thanked you." He stared back at me, his dark eyes penetrating, intense. "Thank you, Walter. Thank you for coming after me."

"I'd never let you go," he said. His cheeks reddened. I wondered if he could hear my heart pounding. For a moment, his eyes held mine and then he headed out the door.

I was relieved to find my cabin empty, no sign of Annie. Light shone through the porthole in a single ray, dust motes floating lazily through it. Like a spotlight, the beam illuminated a circle on the floor. In the middle of the spot of light sat the rectangular box of cards. The miniature coffin—a replica of the chest around which my ghostly ancestors had sat. Their words swam about me, echoing against the timbers. *Pay attention, Lucy,* my father had said, fingering the cards. And Mother: *There's no rush, not now, except for Lucy to learn what she must.* But what—what was it I was supposed to learn? I wondered. And my grandfather—Father's father: *She's our last hope, this one—she and my Pru.* It must mean Pru is alive, I reasoned.

And finally, Mother's words: *It's all in the cards, dear one.*

I knelt and took the cards from the box once more. Spread them across the floor and grouped the face cards. The queen of spades. I held it up to the light, and I swear, her eyes narrowed and her lips curved into a vindictive smile. I quickly turned her facedown on the floor and selected another.

The king of hearts. Familiarity made my heart skip a beat. It was my grandfather—Father's father! I recalled the tired wariness around his eyes, as if exhausted from looking over his shoulder. In fact, he was depicted head on, but the pupils of his eyes peered to the left, watching for something sinister to occur.

The others, I didn't recognize. The spades and clubs were a motley crew of villainous-looking characters. The king of spades held a dagger between his teeth and had a black patch over his right eye. His hair hung beneath a filthy hat, his beard was woven into numerous skinny braids. The king of clubs was equally heinous, a woolly Monmouth cap pulled down so that his thick bushy eyebrows seemed to slink beneath it. A large gold earring hung from one ear and a thick golden chain wrapped several times around his neck. He grasped a sword in his right hand, holding it at a diagonal across his chest.

The red family, to which my grandfather and the sly, dapper card player aboard the specter ship belonged, were of another class altogether. Ladies and gentlemen all, at least in mode of dress. Adorned in velvet and ruffles, some in white wigs and waist-coats, the women in upper-crust finery. The queen of hearts and the red jacks all looked cultured and genteel. The queen of diamonds, though, seemed out of place in her fancy gown. She had a bulldog-like face with angry jowls and small, close-set eyes. A tumble of red curls framed her face. Her mouth was turned in a tight, bitter smile.

"Hmmm . . ." I mused. I paired the face cards this way and that, trying to grasp whatever it was I was supposed to understand.

The ship's bell rang eight times, signaling the end of the afternoon watch and the beginning of the first dog watch. Today that was mine. I collected the cards, careful to keep the queen of spades and king of diamonds separated. I placed all the black face cards together, and tucked them in one side of the box, then did the same with the reds.

But when I placed the queen of diamonds atop her matching king, the card bent and curled in half, then flipped out of my hand. She stared at me from the floor, daring me to pick her up.

I hesitated, then, with thumb and index finger, I gingerly plucked and held her before me. Again, I slowly moved the card back toward the box. The closer I got to the case, from which the king of diamonds smirked, the harder it became. It was as though an invisible hand held me back. I watched the queen's tightly pursed mouth flatten into a straight line.

"What is it?" I asked aloud. "What is it about the king of diamonds?"

I almost jumped out of my skin when the queen of diamonds' lips formed a reply. *The rogue ain't any good! Only got what he deserved!*

Then her face softened. *Too bad the rest of ye has paid fer it too!*

I whispered, "What do you mean?" For a second I saw her actually lean forward off the card, pointing at me with a short, stubby finger.

Beware! Ye could be next! You or yer auntie Pru! But remember—shhhh! Not a word to anyone!

She faded back into her likeness. It floated, as though lifted by the chilly gust that suddenly swept through the cabin, and wafted its way back into the case, inserting itself into the deck far beneath the king of diamonds.

I slammed the lid closed, shoved the box into my bunk beneath the covers, and ran for the door.

12

The morning of my thirteenth birthday I awoke early and peered out the porthole. The dawn was breaking bloodred over the port side of our ship. I slipped my flute into my pocket and tiptoed from the cabin, careful not to disturb Annie, still snoring softly in her bunk. I'd find a peaceful spot and accompany the sunrise with a melody or two.

I'd been counting off the days at sea, in anticipation, and finally, it was here. Thirteen, I thought as I padded quietly through the hall toward the companionway. It felt like a magical number as I rolled it over my tongue. I loved the way it first pursed my lips, then spread them into the beginning of a smile. Three times in a row I whispered the number, savoring the sensation.

I paused at the chart room. What if thirteen *was* a magical number? Feeling charmed, I went inside, moved to the corner, and knelt before Father's safe. Heart pounding, I took the knob in my fingers and turned it carefully right, through the thirties, forties, past zero, climbing through the single digits, then ten, eleven, twelve . . .

Thirteen.

I waited for a click, or some other sign that I was on to something.

Nothing.

Perhaps, I reasoned, it required a combination of trust, insight, and newfound confidence that comes with the age. Or maybe, I thought hopefully, as a birthday gift from beyond, my hand would be supernaturally or otherwise guided. Aunt Pru, I thought, send me some insight! With an open mind, I closed my eyes and spun the dial left until my intuition prompted me to stop, then right, this last revolution undertaken with the care and precision of a surgeon. I would surely feel the mechanism lock into place.

Slowly, slowly, I turned the dial with tense

sweaty fingers. Even more carefully as I approached one complete revolution.

Again, nothing.

Disappointed, I sat back on my heels. Shook my head. Then I stood. I would not, I told myself, let this cast a shadow on my day. I was thirteen. More mature. Well on my way to finding my aunt. Able to weather many things that would have upset me when I was younger and less experienced.

With that I scaled the steps and headed to the poop deck. A peculiar morning it was, the sky a steely gray, with a furling scarlet ribbon of light blazing across the horizon. Off the port side, I spied a distant ship, square-rigged and under full sail, its sharp, black silhouette curiously devilish against the flaming skyline. Even the rhythm of our ship traversing the waves was unusual, adding to the strangeness of the day, her rolling, forward-and-back motion clipped and uneven.

Quaide was at the helm, Georgie beside him. "Hands on the wheel and steady on, mate!" Quaide said, thumping Georgie on the back.

"Steady on!" Georgie repeated, placing his small hands beside Quaide's paws. Grady was on watch. The deck was still slick and glistening from the many canvas buckets of salt water Grady had hauled over the side to wash down her timbers.

As I walked past, he scarcely looked up from tightening the halyards and renipping the buntlines. Ever since I'd gone overboard he'd avoided me. Wouldn't meet my eyes.

"Mornin', Grady," I called.

He mumbled, gesturing toward the sea with his chin, "Red sky at morning . . ." That much I was able to make out. But, of course, I knew the rest of the saying: *Sailors take warning.*

As if in response the mizzen topsail thrashed and thwacked, the spanker gaff snapped. A chill rippled along my back, my arms. I pulled my shirtsleeves down over my knuckles and thrust my hands deep in my pockets. A sudden blast of wind whipped the hair from my face. I felt the curls rise around my head and fly in all directions. Grady chanced a wary glance at me, then away. He shook his head, reciting some mumbo jumbo:

"The Gorgon winged, with snakes for hair—
hated of mortal man—
Medusa, born of the sea . . ."

More superstitious nonsense, I thought, reaching up and harnessing my wild locks. I shivered. Coffee . . . a mug of steaming java would do me good. Heading for the galley, I pulled open the door to the companionway. An unexpected gust flung it from my hand, throwing it back against the wall with a bang.

I grabbed hold, and secured it by slipping the heavy brass hook into the eye attached to the outer wall. The wind whistled through the portal like steam from a teakettle. A feeling of unease crept over me. But it was my birthday. I was thirteen. I wouldn't let a little unsettled weather thwart my special day.

I made my way to the galley, following the scent of the aromatic brew. My stomach growled. Surely Rasjohnny would have some porridge on the stove, and maybe he'd fry me a couple of eggs. This I wanted to quietly enjoy before the rest straggled in for breakfast.

The door to the galley was closed. Perhaps caused by the uncommon rocking of the ship, I reasoned. I placed my hand on the door.

"No, wait!"

I turned. Javan took hold of my arm.

Reading the alarm in his amber eyes, I asked, "What's the matter with you?"

"Not da time to go in dere, no, no," he said, vigorously shaking his head.

"Don't be silly! I'm—"

"Just you be waitin' a little tiny—"

"Javan! I'm hungry!" I shoved his hand away and pushed open the door. Stopped short.

Javan whispered, "Shhhh! Don't be interruptin' him now, missy, stay back!"

Scores of candles set all about the room licked the darkness. Caught by the draft, their flames stretched and dipped in unison like crazed dancers, casting long distorted shadows raving across the ceiling, walls, and floor. In the middle of this, Rasjohnny knelt, keening forward and back, eyes closed, mouth pulled in a tight line. Sweat streamed down his face. A hollow, tuneless hum emanated from his lips. His hands flew, pummeling a small drum, a steady pulse of thrumming that raised the hair on the back of my neck.

"Is he all ri—"

"SHHH!" Javan insisted, his eyes flashing, waving both hands desperately in front of my face. "He's callin' out da *Loa*—da spirits."

I took a step closer, Javan blocking the way. "Please, Miss Lucy, me 'n' you, we go on outta here now, come on!"

My eyes took in a wooden trestle tray of food— dried fruit and fish, and bundles of herbs tied with black string—set to one side of a black canvas mat decorated in geometric shapes of brightly colored crosses and stars. The candlelight caused the images to tremble on the dark field in a foreboding way.

"By the power of the saints, I knew it!" Grady's voice was high and strained. He gripped the edges of the doorframe with white-knuckled fingers, his eyes flashing. "Black magic! That's what yer up to! Knew it the minute this a-cursed day wrestled the night into dawn. Upsettin' the sea and sky itself! Saint Erasmus, save us," he implored, peering skyward. "And lookie!" he exclaimed, pointing a bent arthritic finger at me. "See! In the middle of it, there ye be, missy—I shoulda known as much! All makes sense now, your divin' into the deep. Possessed, I tell ye! The devil's handiwork!"

Heart racing, I followed Grady's gaze. In the center of the mat was a small figure, a doll, about the size of the palm of my hand. It had a flat face crudely carved from wood, sightless eyes of horizontally set cowrie shells. The mouth—a gaping hole—suggested a perpetual silent scream. Hair of dried sea grass streamed wildly from its head, and a makeshift dress woven of the same material covered its body. I gasped. Despite the primitive rendering, I knew from the feeling in my gut who this figure was supposed to be. It was me.

"Nothin' to be a-scared at, miss—no, nothin'!" Javan cried, his words tumbling like waves in a squall. "Don't pay Grady no mind! He don' know 'bout deez dings, he—"

"Cease this devilishness, I tell ye!" Grady roared. "B'fer we all sink to the bottom of the sea and straight to hell!"

Javan pleaded, "Calm down, Grady—you's changin' da flow! Stop!" Grady ignored him, lunged forward, knocked over the tray of food, and viciously kicked the doll from the mat. As his foot connected with her wooden torso a powerful pain caught me in the ribs and I doubled over. Then—an aching lump rose on my forehead as the doll hit the wall.

Rasjohnny slowly emerged from his daze. He stopped drumming. Slumped forward like a scarecrow. His voice went still. I screamed when, in unison, the candles all blew out, my voice lost in the sudden howling of wind and roar of waves. We pitched violently, everything in the room sliding to one side. The ship's bell began to toll relentlessly.

"All hands! All hands!" The cap'n's voice cut through the din. "Batten down the hatches!"

"Say yer prayers!" Grady screamed. He made the sign of the cross, pulled down his cap, and took off running.

13

I ran behind Grady, holding my ribs. My head throbbed. We were tossed against the wall of the companionway, then thrown to the opposite side. With arms extended I pressed on, the pitching of the ship forcing me to climb uphill, then down. Slowly, I zigzagged forward. Marni was already scaling the stairs, clutching the railing. Coleman, silent and determined, stepping into oilskins as he moved, pushed past. The sea rolled and rumbled, relentlessly pounding the ship. Its timbers creaked and groaned. The wind wailed. Annie appeared in the doorway of our cabin.

"Get in there and stay!" I shouted.

"But—"

"In there! Keep Pugsley and Ida! That's your job!" I shoved her in. Slammed the door. "Secure it! Don't come out, no matter what!"

On deck, visibility was next to nothing, but I could still make out the huge whitecaps cresting, churning up a deadly froth. The wind and waves battered us, both attacking from the same direction. "Steady on!" the cap'n hollered. "Lash yourself to the wheel! Run 'er with the wind!" Somehow, through the driving spray, I was able to fight my way to Marni at the helm. I gripped the wheel with her, hand to hand, fist to fist. Our ship's prow sliced through a massive, gun-gray swell. The top of the wave crashed over the rail, coursing across the deck, sucking anything with it that wasn't tied down.

"Strike the royals!" Cap'n shouted. "Strike the royals!"

Three sailors struggled to take down the sails at the top of the masts. More stability without them. Quaide and Grady there, for sure, and Walter—had to be. Or maybe Irish and the Reds. Two more joining the fray—Rasjohnny and Javan. What good Rasjohnny would be, I didn't know, but they worked in tandem. Another, slower but determined, joined them. Addie? Tonio, head tucked and hunkered down, charged across the deck like a bull, laying thick hands to the task. All dark, soaking figures, clad in oilskin, featureless in the rain.

The next surge rose from the side in an undulating peak. It broke diagonally over the stern, thrusting us sideways. A sound emanated from the *Lucy P. Simmons* as though the ship itself took a deep breath and groaned in an effort to stay the course. I lost my footing, fell, and slid, belly down, along the deck. I grabbed for a line, anything to hang on to. On all fours Marni scrambled after me, one hand anchored to a rope, the other extended. Unattended, the wheel spun wildly, knobs ablur. Marni grabbed my hand as the *Lucy P. Simmons* listed dangerously, broadside to the waves. I heard a collective cry as we threatened to capsize. We struggled back to the helm and took hold, every muscle tensing against the wheel, righting her enough to prevent her from broaching.

As our crew doubled its efforts I felt a surge of power manifest itself in the bowels of our ship and stubbornly take charge. On the defensive, its bow sliced through the waves with an air of authority that infused us with courage. The sea retaliated with even more force, rousing the waves to greater heights.

"Strike the topgallants! Strike her down! Abandon course and point!"

The topgallant sails came down, and, like a battering ram, we navigated straight into the wind. Another wall of water, at least twenty feet tall, bore down on us. The sound alone was deafening, ungodly. It filled my ears, blocking out everything else. We rode atop the roiling surface, sucked in by its momentum. So far back did we pitch, it felt we were sailing uphill. But somehow the *Lucy P. Simmons* nosed down and rode the crest of the wave. I battled to stay anchored to the helm, praying the rest could hang on. It was impossible to see, to hear anything but the thunderous sea and howling wind.

The killer surge rose and broke, bombarding us from every direction. It gushed in a tumult across the deck, sucking around our ankles as the ship plunged down the other side of the mountain of raging water. The *Lucy P. Simmons* seemed to inhale and contract, protecting its timbers from the punishing force of the waves.

"Gallants! Strike 'er topsails!" Cap'n screamed. Through the driving rain, pelting my face like liquid nails, I watched the gallants come down. Without most of its sails the ship felt naked, exposed, like a person battling the elements without clothing or protection of any kind. All that was left to power us was the mainsail, full to bursting, then flapping wildly. It was impossible to distinguish sea from sky, the deluge from the waves. The tempest thrashed us horizontally, until the hail began—thousands of icy marbles pounding the deck, bouncing, and rolling, a barrage of frozen bullets. My skin burned under the onslaught.

A sound cut through the din. Or maybe it was inside my head. High and haunting, its lilting strain a mockery. *A la dee dah dah . . . a la dee dah dee . . .* I shook my head to clear the tune away, but still it persisted, until the flute in my pocket took up the chorus. *A la dee dah dah . . . a la dee dah dee . . .*

I looked up, wondering if I was going mad. It happened at sea, Father had told me as much. *A la dee dah dah . . . a la dee dah dee . . .*

Suddenly, I barely noticed the pitch and roll of the ship. Instead, my eyes followed the melody, a sparkling mist of notes that cascaded from my pocket, clearing a narrow tunnel through the wind and water, creating a line of visibility through which I could see. It was like looking through a periscope of calm.

Through it I spied the specter ship hovering just above the ocean, skirting the violent waves. The vicious wind, too, seemed to bypass her, so that she sailed over the fray. Stranger still, she was flying her colors—rows of small, square pennants, in brilliant hues, normally reserved for fair skies and friendly winds. I counted seventeen in all, and then, one by one, deciphered the letters represented by each geometric design.

H–A–P–P–Y–B–I–R–T–H–D–A–Y

L–U–C–Y

I gasped, and in that instant the wind died. The sea became flat as glass. Once more the melody played and quickly faded—*A la dee dah dah. A la dee dah dee*—leaving only the mild lapping of water against the hull. The *Lucy P. Simmons* seemed to sigh and exhale, and then, as if to reassure us, began rocking gently. We all stood in stunned silence for several moments, struggling to believe that the fury had passed as quickly as it had come.

Exhausted, our shoulders slumped, arms drooped at our sides. Muscles quivering. Then the gentle drip-dropping of water trickling from eyebrows and hair, hooded oilskins, the ratlines, yardarms, and mainsail. The sky of grim leaden clouds split down the middle, sending the thunderheads rolling in opposite directions. A wedge of blue emerged between them, through which a ray of golden sun shone. A misty rainbow glittered faintly in a large arc, its ends hidden behind the retreating clouds.

I wiped my face with the back of my hand. Marni's silver hair glistened, hanging down her back in a sleek sheet. Rasjohnny and Javan scrambled from their posts, slipping and sliding across the deck. Quaide was next, methodically descending, rung to rung, jumping the rest of the way, touching down with a thud. Then Grady, quick as a squirrel, Walter behind him. Tonio, his brawny arms hanging at his sides, and Irish, flashing a sparkling smile, pulled off their oilskin hats. The Reds ambled over, thumping each other on their backs, as if they'd played a tough game and emerged victorious. And they had. Even Coleman, in his usual quiet way, looked pleased. Finally, Addie and the cap'n. "Great work, crew," he bellowed. "A hell of a storm!" He ran his hand along the rail, still slick with water. "And a hell of a ship!" The ship's bell clanged in response.

I heard a distant, high-pitched cry. "Can I come out now? Can I?"

Annie!

"Yes!" we yelled, all at once. In a moment she appeared, dog and goat behind her. Pugsley ran circles around us, nose to the ground. My eyes followed him, his restless sniffing raising a creeping anxiety in me.

"Where's Georgie?" I asked.

Rasjohnny, looking pale and spent, just shook his head. "I seed 'im when it first blowed in, out der wid Quaide." He stared at his feet, avoiding our eyes.

"Georgie!" Walter called, striding across the deck. Marni turned toward the rail, her emerald eyes scanning the water like a bird of prey. "Georgie!" Walter shouted again. The men immediately fanned out in all directions, around the perimeter of the ship. My heart pounded in my temples. If he went over . . .

"Quaide," the cap'n barked. "Where's the boy?"

Quaide's eyebrows rose and fell. He chewed his bottom lip. "Yeah, he was out there helpin' me . . . and then . . ." He shrugged. Cap'n's face went white and Quaide burst out laughing. "Come out, ye pea-sized little brute," he yelled. "A regular water rat, that one, runnin' the lines!"

Georgie scurried from behind a barrel that had rolled into the corner, grinning, looking one to the other to acknowledge his joke. Then at Quaide.

Tonio, normally slow moving, turned on his heel, and in a flash was in front of Quaide. His muscular arms were bent at the elbows, fists balled tightly. His mustached lip curled back and he spoke through clenched teeth. "You think that's funny? It's not! I oughta—"

Irish stepped up. "Calm down, Tonio." But the way his black eyes flashed at Quaide you could see he agreed. Quaide smirked. I wanted to slap him.

"None o' yas got any sense o' humor."

The Reds stood, mouths gaping, looking one to the other, shaking their heads. One of them muttered, "Ain't no kinda joke." Coleman rolled his shoulders and took a step back. His nostrils flared as though he'd gotten a whiff of a three-day-old fish.

Marni looked from Addie to Georgie. "Miss Addie," she said, her voice unusually soft but strong, "take Master Georgie to his cabin." Georgie started to protest, but Marni shot him a look that clipped his tongue. "Cap'n!" she said.

Cap'n glared at Quaide. "Now. You, me, Miss Marni. My stateroom." He turned on his heel and strode off. Stopped. Pointed. "What are all of you looking at? There's work to be done! Snap to it!"

The men stood there for a second more, then headed to their stations. All except Walter, who followed Marni and the cap'n. Grady paused beside me. "I guess happy birthday greetings are in order." He was not smiling. His eyes were narrowed and he stepped so close we were nearly eye to eye. I could see the pores on his nose, small black dots like pinpricks. He dropped his voice to a hoarse whisper.

"I seen that specter ship out there, flyin' her colors. Sendin' birthday wishes your way. A pitiable irony, it is. A curse, I tell ye . . . Between that and the other one's black magic, it's a miracle we got us through it. That wasn't no natural storm. Not just some whip-tail end of a hurrycane." He turned on his heel and stalked off, as if the whole ordeal had been my doing. Had it, somehow, been my fault? Was the queen of spades flexing her muscles again as a warning—to remind me not to speak of what I'd experienced overboard?

I sunk against the side of the poop deck and peered out over the ocean, now a tranquil bath of blue-green. I shielded my eyes from the sparkling pellets of hail that still clung to her timbers, as though encrusted with thousands of crystal beads. Scanning the horizon, there was no sign of the specter ship, and, for that matter, no sign of the black square-rigged vessel I'd seen earlier. The specter ship—well, that was another story, but the black vessel—I wondered if it'd survived the storm, or if it had been swallowed up and brought to the bottom of the sea. I pulled my spyglass from my pocket and peered out, north, south, east, west. Nothing.

My stomach growled and churned, but I wasn't ready to venture back into the galley. By now

Rasjohnny must have rushed to hide the evidence of his ritual, whatever it was, but still I hesitated. We couldn't pretend I hadn't seen. Something ought to be said, but what? Sighing, I headed to my own cabin.

I slipped down the stairs, still wet and slick, along the companionway. Voices could be heard farther down the corridor, coming from the cap'n's stateroom. I wasn't eavesdropping—I didn't need to. Anyone here would have heard. Raised voices, the cap'n's and Walter's. An indiscernible grunt I knew belonged to Quaide. Marni's voice, low and measured. I slipped silently along the wall.

"Stay away from him!" Walter shouted. "He's just a kid. You're not a good influence!"

"Just payin' him some attention," Quaide said. "From a *real* sailor. Don't have a father. Can't get it from 'is brother."

I felt the punch of his words.

"Everyone aboard this ship is a real sailor," the cap'n snapped. "Don't forget it."

"Yeah," Quaide drawled, "but Wally here puts all 'is attention on the girl. Got nothin' left fer the kid." He raised his voice to a high, fluttering pitch. "He's love struck. Smitten!"

"That isn't true!" Walter said with vehemence. There was a scuffling sound.

"Sit down, Walter," Marni said gently. My face burned. Was it true, that Walter was smitten, or was Quaide, that animal, just trying to goad Walter into ignoring me?

"Somebody's gotta pay the kid some mind," Quaide persisted flatly.

"That's all," Marni barked. "We've heard quite enough from you!"

"Well, Quaide," the cap'n said. "I didn't realize that child welfare was something you championed. The boy has family and friends aboard this ship. And they don't include you, is that clear? You exercised extremely poor judgment today. The lad is impressionable and I won't have you leading him astray. Period. Steer clear of him!"

"Thank you, Cap'n," Marni said.

I turned on my heel and moved quickly to my cabin. Once inside it took a moment for my eyes to adjust to the dim light. I'd begun the day with such high hopes that thirteen would be different. And it was—but not in the ways I'd hoped. Voodoo, a violent squall, Quaide's taunting of Walter being smitten with me. I sighed and headed toward my bunk, bone tired.

A faint clattering sound stopped me. A rat in the cabin, escaping rising water in the bilge? I froze, trying to determine the source. There, in the corner—no—it was from Annie's berth. I grabbed a thick book off the shelf to hurl at it. *Cl . . . cl . . . cl . . . clackclackclack . . . clclclclclclclclcl . . . . CLACK!* I reached back and opened the door to provide an escape route for the vermin. Crept toward the bunk.

I peered into the tangled nest of blankets. Silence. Then *cl . . . cl . . . cl . . .* The covers shifted. I raised the copy of *Treasure Island*. Aimed. Took a deep breath and heaved it.

Nothing. I tiptoed forward.

Cl . . . cl . . . cl . . . cl . . . Like chattering teeth . . . or were they mine? I craned my neck. Bit my lip.

CLACK!

I pinched the edge of the blanket and yanked it up in the air.

The black box of cards. The lid trembled and shook. *Cl . . . cl . . . cl . . . POP!*

The top blew off and the deck shot out. A shower of cards floated toward my feet. They landed in a pyramid arrangement, a house of cards that looked suspiciously like our mansion back at Simmons Point—before it became a ship. There, the porch, there, a turret. The cards facing out were face cards, all of the characters I'd seen aboard the specter ship. Plus the image of Mother and Father in the upstairs windows.

I gaped at them.

They all leaned forward, their mouths moving in unison.

"Happy birthday, Lucy!" Mother blew a kiss. Father saluted. Then the queen of spades threw back her head and laughed, a long, sarcastic cackling, until the house of cards blew in on itself and collapsed in a heap.

14

The tail ends of dreams swam through my head like a school of dark fish, swishing their slick bodies inside my brain. . . . A rat beneath my blankets with chattering teeth, nibbling my toes. The cowrie-eyed voodoo doll stalking across the deck. Giant playing cards bobbing in the ocean like flotsam. Quaide, hooking something from the sea, hauling it up on a squeaky winch. Dangling from the line, it dripped. As it spun, back to front, I saw it was a face card. And the face on the card was mine. I woke up. Sat bolt upright in my bunk, disoriented. Sweating. A shaft of early afternoon sunlight cast a warm beam through the cabin. Hard to believe that just this morning a storm had been raging.

The cards! I looked toward the floor where they'd fallen. The box sat on the bunk, cards neatly stacked inside. Had the house of cards been part of my dream? Or had it actually happened?

Knock knock knock. I shook my head to clear away the nightmare images. *Knock knock.* Someone was at the door. I swung my feet to the floor. Shivering, I realized I'd never changed out of my wet clothes—after the drama with Quaide and the house of cards, I must have sunk back to my bunk and fallen right off to sleep.

"Lucy!"

I wrapped myself in a blanket and threw open the door.

"Happy birthday, Lucy!"

They were all there—Addie in front, a lopsided cake on a platter in her outstretched hands. A parcel wrapped in paper, tied with string, was tucked beneath her arm. Hours later they still all looked a little green and disheveled from the storm, but their smiles more than made up for it.

"Can't believe me girl is thirteen!" Addie gushed. *Tirteen* is how it sounded.

Annie threw herself against me and wrapped her arms around my legs. Georgie grinned sheepishly.

"We got presents for you!" he said. He held a burlap sack in his clenched fist.

Marni smiled with one side of her mouth, eyeing what must have been my frightening appearance. "Glad to see you dressed up for your party!" I ran a hand through my damp, salt-encrusted hair and pulled the blanket more tightly around me, suddenly embarrassed. There was Walter at the back of the group. When our eyes met he nodded and looked away. So, this is how it will be, I thought, feeling something between sadness and anger. All thanks to Quaide.

"Well then," Addie cried happily, "I say we give Lucy a minute or two to freshen herself up." She winked at me and continued. "Then meet in Miss Marni's stateroom for the proper party to begin!"

"Yes, lovely." I found myself having to push some levity into my voice in order not to show my frustration about Walter.

"Go on then," Addie ordered, handing the cake off to Marni. "I've somethin' special t' give. The rest o' ye go on ahead!" They turned and headed for the stateroom. Annie stuck her blond head back in the doorway.

"And Lucy . . ." Her blue eyes were open wide. "Hurry up!"

Addie stepped in and closed the door behind

her. "A heck of a day it 'twas!" she exclaimed, "but fittin', somehow, for one as lively and brave as me little Lucy. How grand it will be for your auntie t' see how the sense of adventure she's always had runs in the fam'ly!" Her face beamed with pride.

My heart instantly filled to overflowing. "Addie..." I began. My eyes welled up and I stopped. There was so much I hadn't told her. "Everything is ... different.... There's so much ..."

"Aye," she said, "the teen years are like that, they are, fer sure."

"It isn't that.... It's ... you know, when I fell overboard ..." I stopped. Bit my tongue.

"Don't be frettin' about that, child. It turned out fine, now didn't it?" She held out the parcel. "Here ... I've been preparin' fer this day fer quite a while, I 'ave."

Addie watched me take the parcel and untie the string. I folded back the brown paper, revealing a patch of beautiful pine-green satin. It shimmered as I ran a finger along it. The paper fell away, and a gorgeous frock unfurled. It had a sweet-heart neckline, trimmed in delicate black lace, a waist cinched with a matching thick band of black velvet. The sleeves, also of black lace, puffed slightly at the shoulder and fell in an airy flounce just below the elbow. Black velvet bows edged the sleeves. The bodice was shirred black satin with twinkling green crystal buttons down the front.

"Addie . . . it's beautiful! Where did you . . ."

"Bought the fabric in Boston town, I did. Been stitchin' by lamplight durin' the evenin's ev'ry chance I got." The pleasure on her face warmed me, and also conjured up a wave of sadness. How I would have loved for Mother . . . "Oh, Addie, it's so beautiful!" I placed the dress on Annie's bunk and threw myself at her. We embraced, until she grabbed my shoulders and held me at arm's length.

"Go on to the head. I poured ye some water in the basin and left some Pear's soap, scented with lavender, 'tis. Wash yerself up. Then come back and we'll get ye all gussied up!" She leaned close and whispered. "I bet I know someone aboard this ship who can't wait to see the young lady in her finery! Go on! Go!"

As I went to the head, I wondered if Walter would look up long enough to notice. Inside, I dropped the blanket, peeled off my wet clothes, and shivered again as I dunked my arms in the basin. I lathered up with the bar of lavender soap, washed as best I could, and rinsed. Looked into the small oval mirror tacked to the wall. A cloudy image stared back at me, so like my aunt Pru. The Simmons eyes, the wild red hair. Face slimmer than it had been in childhood. My heart tripped with longing—and determination.

Back in the cabin, Addie helped me into my dress, then brushed my hair from my face in long, torturous strokes. She wrapped and coiled and tucked and pinned. I bit my tongue, as complaints would seem juvenile.

"There. Now, step back and let me have a look at ye!"

I spun in a circle, afraid to move my head for fear of upsetting my coiffure.

"Ye look like a dream, ye do! Now, just loosen up yer neck, so's ye don't appear like a wooden pilin' in a dress!"

In the short time it took for us to march to the stateroom, I became aware of just how comfortable I'd become in denim overalls. The gorgeous dress pinched at the waist and the crinoline underneath it pricked my skin. And, despite what Addie had said, I felt myself holding my neck very rigid in order to preserve my complicated hairstyle. We passed the Reds in the companionway. Their four blue eyes popped in unison and they stepped aside. One, then the other bowed deeply. "M'lady . . ." said the first. "Yer wish is our command," said the second. I blushed, and covered the smile on my lips with my hand. Laughed out loud as I noticed the black lines ground under my fingernails—a permanent state of affairs since becoming an expert at all the duties and chores aboard ship.

Addie pushed open the stateroom door. *"TAH DAH!"* she announced as I swept in. Annie squealed in delight and rushed over, touching my skirts with tentative hands and extended pinkies. "Oooh . . . Princess Lucy!" she cooed.

"That ain't Lucy," Georgie said skeptically, peering at me as though he'd never seen me before.

"Isn't," Marni stressed. "That *isn't* Lucy."

"Then who is it?" Georgie asked, missing the point. He was starting to sound more and more like Quaide.

Marni gazed at me, the edges of her mouth twitching. "What a vision!" she exclaimed. I couldn't help looking at Walter. "Happy birthday, Lucy," he mumbled, his Adam's apple bobbing, cheeks flushed. He looked away in an instant.

"Cake or present first?" Marni asked.

"Cake!" Georgie shouted.

"Present," insisted Annie.

"Lucy?" Marni asked.

"Present," I said. Georgie thrust the burlap bag at me. It was light, whatever it was. I reached in and felt a smooth surface with soft edges. A book of some kind.

"Take it out! Come on!" Georgie urged.

I pulled out a slender volume. The title read, *Fingering and Embouchure Technique for Flute and Recorder.*

"I found it in my chest of drawers," Marni said. "Thought you could use it to learn some new songs. We've all heard that one you play—and only part of it, to boot! Now . . . who knows . . . you might learn a whole repertoire of sea chanteys!"

I opened the book. It was filled with staves of scale-wise notes, and beneath each, a crude drawing of a flute, some holes open and others darkened. There were numbers beneath each ranging from 1 to 4.

"The darkened circles show where to place your fingers to produce the note pictured." Marni pointed to the diagrams. "The numbers indicate which fingers to use."

"This is wonderful!" I said, thinking of the book of sea chanteys I had stowed in my room. "Thank you, Marni, thank you all!"

Georgie pleaded, "Now can we have cake?"

Marni laughed and turned toward the tray laden with cake and plates, took the silver cutter, and held it high.

"Make a wish," Walter said. He looked up at me for just a moment, his eyes bright. Marni waited.

"All right," I said, and closed my eyes. The words jumped into my mind. I wish Walter wouldn't pay Quaide any mind, so we can go on as we had before. I opened my eyes and stared at Walter, to see if my wish had taken hold. But he kept his eyes on his brother. Marni looked at me, questioningly. I nodded, feeling rather deflated, as she sliced the first wedge. Addie helped her pass the pieces around. I plunged my fork in and savored the sweet yellow cake, spiced with cinnamon and cardamom. But the sweetness couldn't remove the hint of bitterness I felt toward Walter. That, and the thought that I'd wasted a wish. Why hadn't I wished for . . . safety at sea, success in finding Aunt Pru, unlocking the safe and the mystery of the family curse? No. Instead, I wished for some silly boy to notice me. I'd show him!

There was a tap on the door and I pushed past Walter to open it. Rasjohnny stood bearing a large tray of coffee and milk.

"Refreshments for de birt'day girl, I got!" He ducked through the doorway, his dark eyes searching my face. He moved past and set the tray on the sideboard.

"Why not send for Javan?" I asked. "He'd love to have some cake, I'm sure." Walter shot me a surprised look and quickly turned away. My heart skipped a beat. Had it been a brief flash of jealousy I detected? I was almost ashamed at the satisfaction I felt.

Georgie, his chin covered in crumbs, mumbled, "I'll go get 'im." He pressed his index finger onto the remaining morsels of cake on his dish, licked his finger clean, and fetched two more plates. "I'll bring this to 'im," he said.

Walter stepped in front of him. "Good idea. Bring Javan a slice of cake. But what do you think you're doing with that second piece?"

Perhaps Walter preferred Javan not join our party. And secondly, I'm sure he imagined Georgie sneaking Quaide the extra slice. Marni and Walter exchanged a glance. "Leave the plates here," Marni said, "and bring Javan back. That's all."

Georgie set the plates down with a clatter, hunched his shoulders, and huffed toward the door. Walter reached out, placing a hand on his brother's shoulder. Georgie shrugged it off. "Georgie!" Walter said, but he was already on his way. I fought the feeling of empathy that rose in my chest. I walked to the door and watched Georgie go. Rasjohnny bent to exit, and as he did our eyes met.

"A word widdya, miss?" He mouthed the words. "Soon as ya can make it t' da kitchen, yes?" I tried to avoid his eyes, still feeling so unsettled from the scene in the galley. But the begging in his voice tugged at me. He whispered, "Gotta explain, I do." The others were laughing and talking, enjoying their dessert, pouring coffee. I slipped out the doorway and closed the door quietly behind me.

"Rasjohnny . . . what were you doing this morning? The candles, the doll . . ."

"I pray dat ye didn't tell . . . and Grady, he be too superstitional."

"I didn't tell, not yet. But I should . . ."

"No, please, Miss Lucy, the cap'n might be misunderstandin', and Miss Marni."

"Lucy! Where'd ye slip off ta?" It was Addie's voice.

"Be right there, Addie. Would you pour me some coffee?"

Rasjohnny turned, throwing furtive glances this way and that. "Ya see, back on my island, me, I be da shaman. I feels dings of da spirit world. And sence you fell overboard, well, da spirits be twitchy. Restless. I feels it, here." He patted his chest with an open hand. "It be da spirits called you into da waters, yes, it be true."

I felt my mouth go dry. He pressed on. "So, Rasjohnny, I calls da Loa, da spirits of good to protect you. Just in case. Not black magic like Grady say."

"Lucy!"

"Coming, Addie! Just a minute!"

"You believe me?"

I stared at his dark eyes, his halo of tiny braids, full lips. There was nothing in his demeanor that suggested anything but caring. Nothing in his words that rang false. In fact, he'd sensed what no one else, save Marni perhaps, had suspected about my plunge into the sea.

He sighed, and I realized he took my silence as an unspoken no. "Miss Lucy—"

"Yes," I whispered. "Yes, I guess I do believe you." I hesitated, trying to think of how to phrase my next question.

"I hears a 'but' in your voice. . . ."

I took a deep breath. "If you're a shaman, you must know about magic, right? I mean, where it comes from, if it's good or bad?"

"Ah," he said, considering. "Magic—it be a mystery. Like love. Like death. Pow'ful stuff, deez myst'ries! It ain't t' understand, much as to respect it. Some's dey got eyes to see it comin', some's blind."

I considered this—thought about how some of us fully recognized the peculiarities of the specter ship. Coleman did, and certainly Grady. Marni and Walter. Addie. Annie. The cap'n. Javan. But the rest seemed to perceive only what seemed reasonable. Maybe Rasjohnny was right—you needed the eyes to see. "But the magic . . . is it bad, or is it good?"

"Why you askin' bout good 'n' bad? Open dem eyes. Just like wid folks in da world. If what dey's doin' bring bout good, dey's good. If what dey's doin' bring about bad, dey's bad. Same wid magic. See what it done, den ya know if it be good or evil. Fact dat you standin' here look pretty good t' me. . . ."

My hand went to my aching ribs, the lump on my head. Rasjohnny nodded. "Dat, danks to Grady, gettin' in da middle of it."

Georgie appeared, running at full tilt, Javan following behind him.

Rasjohnny met my eyes, blinked slowly, then headed back toward the galley. The cabin door opened. I turned around and came face to face with Walter. My heart thumped. He'd come looking for me after all.

Georgie clamored through the portal and I stared up into Walter's face, a smile playing on my lips.

But as much as I willed it, he didn't meet my gaze. His eyes shifted to some point above my right shoulder. I turned to see Javan standing behind me, hands in his pockets, a lazy smile playing across his lips.

"Time for my watch," Walter mumbled, pushing

past. Javan shrugged and loped into the cabin, his eyes fixed on the lovely frosted torte awaiting him.

I watched Walter go, feeling suddenly ridiculous in my fancy dress, and even more foolish for thinking he'd notice.

15

Back in my cabin I peeled off my frock, which had, to my mind, lost much of its luster. I hung it carefully in the armoire, silently thanking Addie for her efforts, even though I clearly could not do the dress justice. I'd no sooner pulled on my cotton work shirt and overalls when Annie and Pugsley tumbled in, followed by Ida.

"Why'd you take off your beautiful gown?" Annie asked.

"Didn't want to dirty it," I lied. I grabbed my flute, my birthday book of *Fingering and Embouchure Technique for Flute and Recorder*, and my old crumbling volume of sea chanteys. I needed something to lose myself in, and the finer points of the music might be just the thing. The songs I was able to play consisted of only a handful of notes. I decided I'd learn the names and finger positions of all of them.

Annie chirped, "Ooh—will you teach me too?"

"Once I learn it!" I felt snappish with her, and ashamed of myself. But she didn't notice, taking my words at face value.

I flipped open the new book and stared from the diagrams to my flute. Hole to hole, they matched. I stretched and plied the fingers of my left hand, anchored with my thumb, carefully covering each opening, as indicated. T for the thumb, 1 for my index finger, on to the middle fingers, 2 and 3. Then, the fingers of my right hand, all in a row, 1, 2, 3, 4, with a couple of tiny holes for the pinkie. Each corresponded to a note with a letter name. I tipped my fingers so that the soft pad of flesh on my fingertip completely concealed the opening. It wasn't as easy as it looked.

I stared at the diagram and tried it several times without blowing into the shaft, watching to be sure my fingers formed an airtight seal, then lifting one, then the next, until all the top holes were open. Then I put it to my lips. *Hoot ... hoot ... hoot ... hoot ... hoot.* I did it with only a slight waver between the G and the A notes. I was so focused I forgot Annie and Pugsley sitting beside me, hanging on every reedy sound, until Pugsley raised his flat snout and howled.

I moved from one note to the next, and the do-re-mi-fa-sol flowed. One by one I learned the rest of the notes by adding my pinkie, then the fingers of my right hand—low C, D, E, and F, and by covering, then uncovering, each hole, bottom to top. As I mastered this, a colorful cloud of mist rose from the instrument, floating, in increments, with each ascending note.

"Oh my!" Annie whispered. "Lucy—you're playing a rainbow! I want to learn that too!"

I smiled at her and continued practicing, following the patterns and finger numbers, producing a range of pitches. The colorful mist danced merrily, larger bursts when I played greater intervals, cascades for ascending or descending scale tones.

Feeling confident, and having mastered these simple patterns, I turned the page and learned still more combinations. Each new note changed the color of the magical mist, shooting off bursts of fuchsia and teal, copper and silver. Annie oohed and ahhed. Side by side, I compared the fingering and note chart to my book of sea chanteys. It would take a lot of practice to become proficient enough to produce the correct notes in time. And certainly more patience than I had at the moment.

I was about to hand the flute off to Annie to give her a try, but my elbow locked, and the flute remained stubbornly in front of me. I moved it from my lips and it persistently flew back toward my mouth. My heart began to race as I realized I was, once again, being led by a mysterious force. On its own, a melody tumbled from the instrument, over and over again. My fingers were sucked to the tone holes, pulled into the pattern of the repeated snippet of song. Over and over it repeated, until I knew it by heart, the soft pads of each finger sore. The melody always ended on the same pitch. I looked at the chart.

D. It ended always on the low D. Heavily, deliberately, the emphasis on the D as if saying, "I told you so!"

Then, something peculiar happened. With my fingers hypnotized, still repeating the tune, the flute began to move. I had no choice but to follow.

"Where are you going, Lucy?" Annie asked. I tried to pull my lips away in order to answer, but they too were under the spell. I felt like the Pied Piper, marching out the doorway and along the hall, tootling the notes in triplets—D–D–F, A–G–F, G–E–C, D . . .

A parade followed—Annie, Pugsley, and Ida—Annie in the lead, skipping in 6/8 time, humming along. We passed Javan in the hallway. Upon seeing the glittering waves of music, his amber eyes widened and his mouth fell open. "Miz Lucy—I's think you learnt to conjure the Loa!"

"Come on," Annie cried. "It's magic music!" Javan's shocked expression turned into a grin and he joined the spectacle.

The tenacious tune drew me along the hallway. The tempo increased as we neared the chart room, puffs of dazzling vapor in jewel-like shades creating a fireworks display. The glittering mist seeped around and beneath the chart-room door, and without so much as a nudge of my foot, the portal opened. Faster and faster my fingers flew over the notes, stronger and stronger became the invisible current that dragged me inside. The melody slowed as it led me to the corner where Father's safe taunted me. The flute dipped, pulling me to my knees before the locked strongbox. The tempo decreased, dramatically ending on the D note. That final tone sounded until every last ounce of breath was expended, and I went limp as a jellyfish. My hands finally relaxed and dropped from the instrument, which, of its own accord, waggled and danced before the safe, sounding the D one more time like an encore. Annie and Javan applauded. I sat there exhausted, the tune still running through my head, when the ship's bell sounded, signaling the beginning of the first dog watch—it was four o'clock. "That's my watch," I said. There would still be plenty of repairs to do after the beating we took in the storm, every sail carefully examined, frayed ropes repaired or replaced. There was rigging to be tarred, and sticky oakum fibers to be pressed between the timbers of the deck, resealing her surfaces.

"Leave the flute with me," Annie begged.

Javan chimed in. "We want a turn!"

I stood on shaky knees. Against their protests I tucked the instrument into my pocket. "I'll bet you'll see some dolphins doing tricks after the storm," I said. "You should go and see. Go on!" They stood for a moment, eyeing me carefully, perhaps waiting to see if they'd miss one last burst of glitter. Ida tipped her head quizzically and Pugsley whined, his curly tail wagging. Annie shrugged and ran off, Pugsley and Ida behind her.

Javan lingered. "My ol' man, he said it, and I can see it's true. Da spirits don' sleep 'board dis ship. 'Tween you, and him, and Miz Marni . . . yas bring out a lotta good magic!" Javan grinned, a smile no less brilliant than the glittering music. "Gotta get back to work!" He turned and was gone, leaving me alone in the chart room. I glanced back at the safe and the flute purred in my pocket. What was it trying to tell me? I left the room through the companionway, and on toward my chores. It would be good to scrub and pound, swab and scour. Mindless tasks that required brawn, not brains.

I joined Irish, who acknowledged me with a nod, and began pounding oakum into each crevice. Side by side we worked. He whistled a Celtic ditty lightly through his teeth, but all I heard was D–D–F, A–G–F, G–E–C, D. . . . It was a nagging refrain, an annoying fly, a mosquito in my ear. The ship, cruising along smoothly at about eight knots, dipped and rolled in time. No matter how much elbow grease I used, how much concentration and effort I afforded the task, how many blisters I wore into my fingertips, the tune persisted. I decided to join the Reds, hoping a change of scene might interrupt the incessant melody, or enlighten me to its meaning.

As I crossed the deck I spied Grady, wedge-shaped sextant in hand, squinting through the eyepiece, measuring the angle between the sun and the horizon. He put the instrument aside, scribbled something on a scrap of paper, then went back to it. His movements were jerky. Agitated. After each coordinate recorded, he shook his head, tipped it to one side, narrowed his eyes, and scanned the skyline. Yanked off his denim cap, mopped his brow, slapped it back on his head. "It ain't right," he grumbled. "Don't add up." The lines, straining under full sail, squeaked and yawled like a peal of laughter.

"What's wrong?" I asked. Grady frowned, then spun about, glaring at me. "By all calculations, by dead reckoning, we ain't where we supposed to be."

I knew the cap'n had abandoned course in order to cooperate with the angry seas. "The storm pushed us astray?" I asked.

Grady peered off into the distance, chewing his bottom lip, rubbing thumbs and index fingers together. "No storm could've thrown us this far. No regular storm, anyway."

My stomach fell. This would add time to our voyage. Slow us down. "How much time will we need to make up?"

Grady snorted. "Make up? Makin' up time ain't the issue."

"What do you mean? You just said . . ."

"I knows what I said. We didn't lose time. We gained it. We can forgit reprovisioning in the Azores. Passed 'em by completely, and Cape Verde as well!"

I did a quick calculation—Boston to the Azores should take about sixteen days, maybe more, then a week to Cape Verde. "But that's impossible!"

"Exactly my point," Grady growled. "Ain't possible for a God-fearing seaman aboard a *normal* vessel. But with all the devilishness goin' on here . . ."

"So, where are we, exactly?"

He shook his head, dubious. "By all accounts—about a couple of days outside a St. Helena—South Atlantic, case you don't know."

"That means we'll be rounding the Cape of Good Hope . . ."

"Much sooner than we woulda."

"But that's wonderful news!" I exclaimed. If what he said was true, we'd gained over a week! Again, as if in agreement, the lines squealed and her sails flapped like a round of applause. Grady glared, spit, and stalked off, muttering under his breath. A smile spread across my face. It was a birthday gift—the storm! That much closer to finding Aunt Pru! I looked up at my ship's majestic masts, at her sails puffed proudly before the wind. "Thank you!" I shouted, waving a fist in the air.

I skipped over to the Reds.

"Help?" I asked. They nodded and tossed me a chamois cloth.

"Glad t' see you're not sportin' your lovely

frock out here," one of them said.

The other chuckled. "She's savin' it for a grand fete when we get to the down under. An Outback Ball!"

I grinned and rolled up my sleeves. D–D–F, A–G–F, G–E–C, D . . . I hummed the tune in spite of myself as I scoured the rail, making my way from the main deck toward the poop deck. Sailing at such a good clip produced a refreshing breeze, and that, with the snap and flap of its sails, the happy creak and groan of her planking, and the steady swish and roll of her bow, was music to a seafarer's ears.

Abruptly a peculiar sound behind me cut through my reverie. Harsh laughter, and then a voice: "B-neet, b-neet, b . . . b . . . b . . . b-neet." More laughter. "B-b-b-b-b-neet, b-neet, b . . . b . . . b . . . b-neet."

Then another voice. "Come on, spit it out! You can do it!" The voice was Quaide's.

I turned and tiptoed forward. Ducked behind the lifeboat and peered toward the bow.

Coleman stood, his face pale, hair ruffling like downy feathers in the breeze. Quaide, his hulking back to me, poked the man's thin wiry frame with a thick finger. "Cat got yer tongue? Tell me where you're goin'!" Coleman's lips labored in slow motion, as if paralyzed. His jaw stretched painfully. He thrust his head forward, the sinews in his neck straining.

"B . . . b . . . b . . ." His nostrils flared. Hands fisted and unfisted. "B . . . b . . . b . . . b-neet . . ."

Quaide closed the space between them. Thrust his doughy face directly in front of Coleman's. "Come on, say it, you moron! Out with it! You gotta tell your superior what you're gonna be doin'. And that's me! So *say it*!"

Coleman tried to scoot around him. Quaide blocked his way.

I felt weak in the knees. I'd never actually heard Coleman speak, assuming he was just an odd, solitary sort. It never occurred to me he was a stutterer.

"Say it . . . *BE-NEATH* . . . say it! *BILGE PUMP!*" I could see the spit fly from Quaide's lips. Coleman clamped his mouth shut like a steel trap, vehemently shook his head. His chest rose and fell with each breath.

I lowered my head, heart pounding. I was about to shout at Quaide, but stopped. I couldn't bear for Coleman to know I'd witnessed this.

I turned. Ran to get the cap'n. He wasn't anywhere on deck, so I hurried below, toward his stateroom. "Cap'n!" I shouted. "Cap'n Adams!" I pounded on his door.

"Cap'n, I need you on deck! Cap'n!"

The cap'n's door flew open. Marni, hearing the ruckus, also stepped out of her quarters. Before I could say another word, Irish bolted down the companionway and into the corridor. "It's Quaide," he said, huffing and puffing. He raked a hand through his jet-black hair and caught his breath. "Stabbed. Quaide's been stabbed!"

16

We ran, the sound of our footsteps echoing in the companionway like a drumroll.

The men stood in a circle on deck, their backs to us. All I could see of Quaide were the bottoms of his massive boots, toes up.

Grady barked, "Let Cap'n through!" Tonio and the Reds stepped aside. Rasjohnny was barreling toward us, a large black bag in hand. Addie appeared, and with a single glance grabbed Annie and yanked her back into the companionway.

Cap'n shouted, "Clear a space!" He was already kneeling at Quaide's side, waving Rasjohnny in. I wedged my way between them, hypnotized by the red, soggy stain spreading across Quaide's right shoulder. He was struggling to sit up, but Cap'n pushed him down and peeled back his shirt. Rasjohnny examined the wound, dabbed with a cloth. Quaide winced.

"He gonna be fine, just fine," Rasjohnny said. "Ain't deep."

Georgie ran forward. "Quaide!" he yelled. Georgie looked from Quaide to Walter, and everyone's eyes followed. My heart raced as I read the suspicion on his young face, the hurt and indignation on Walter's. Marni stepped forward, placed a firm hand on Georgie's shoulder, quieting him.

Cap'n scanned the group and flew to his feet. "Where's Coleman?" He snapped his fingers. "Grady! Irish! Tonio! Find him. I need all hands on deck! All hands!" he shouted. "Everyone accounted for! Now!"

Grady, Tonio, and Irish dashed off. A sick feeling rose in my throat.

"Quaide," the cap'n said, "what happened? Speak up!"

Sweat beaded across Quaide's forehead. His bottom lip curled down, revealing the fleshy inside, white and plump as a fat grub. He chewed his upper lip, ran his thick fingers through his hair, eyelids at half-mast.

"Was pretty worn out after the storm. Come up

to the poop deck for a look-see—makin' sure every-thin' was in order. Sat down against the rail for a minute and I musta nodded out. Woke up bleedin' like a pig."

The cap'n's eyebrows arched. "You're saying nothing happened out there on the poop deck? That someone stabbed you while you slept? Unpro-voked?"

Quaide grunted. "I'm sayin' I woke up with this. Didn't see nothin'—was in shock." He paused. "Heard footsteps runnin' off . . ."

"He's lying!" I shouted.

Quaide glared at me, his teeth showing. "You're the little liar," he growled through clamped teeth. "You wasn't there!"

All eyes were on me.

"What happened, Lucy?" Marni's calm voice eased my anxiety. "What exactly did you see?"

Nostrils flaring, I turned to Quaide. Glanced at Cap'n, who nodded.

"He—Quaide," I pointed, "was tormenting Coleman. Up on the deck, forward, near the bow. Humiliating him!"

"Ain't so—" Quaide began.

"Quiet!" the cap'n snapped. "Go on, Miss Lucy."

I took a deep breath, gritted my teeth. "He was . . . he was . . . trying to force Coleman to speak, and Coleman just couldn't. He was stuttering.

Stammering. Quaide laughed, kept pushing him."
I could still hear the rapid-fire *b-b-b-b-nee* . . . could
still see Coleman's twisted face. I forced the qua-
ver from my voice. Looked Cap'n Adams in the eye.
"That's when I came to get you. To make him stop!"

"So you didn't see anyone stabbed?"

My hands were shaking. Without meaning to,
I'd cast suspicion on Coleman. There was no one
else around.

"She didn't see nothin'," Quaide muttered.

"I saw you behaving like an animal!" I hissed.
I stopped myself before I spoke my mind . . . *You
deserved to get stabbed.* I was appalled at my own
thought.

"We found 'im, Cap'n," Grady announced, walking beside Tonio and Irish, Coleman loping between
them, eyes cast downward. "Pumpin' the bilge."

"Irish. Tonio. Escort Coleman to my quarters," Cap'n Adams ordered. "Miss Marni, Lucy,
you too. Rasjohnny—bring Quaide to the galley.
Stitch him up. Grady. Walter. Reds. Sail this ship.
Grady, see that everyone stays at his station. No one
belowdecks. Now—everyone—get to it!"

Georgie wailed, "I'm goin' with Quaide!"

The cap'n retorted, "No, young man, you are
not. You'll go with your brother. Your hands are
needed. Move!"

We marched to Cap'n Adams's stateroom. "Sit

down, all of you," he said. He directed Marni and me to pull forward two chairs, sat behind his desk, and waved Coleman into a seat opposite him. Coleman wrung his hands.

"Coleman," the cap'n said. His voice was soft but hard as iron. "Did you or did you not stab Quaide? Look at me!"

Coleman met the cap'n's determined gaze. Shook his head vehemently side to side. His eyes appeared sunken in his face, cheeks hollow. His mouth convulsed painfully, in slow motion. Cap'n tore a page from his log, thrust it, along with a whittled pencil, across the desk. "I need to know what happened."

Coleman grasped the pencil between thumb and middle finger, and began to write. His lips pursed with the formation of each word. Marni and I leaned forward. From his long, awkward hand came the most surprisingly graceful script:

Quaide ordered me to go beneath—pump the bilge.

He glanced up and back to the page. *That's what I did. Went beneath to the bilge pump. Then they came for me.*

"And how exactly did Quaide deliver these orders?"

Coleman looked away. Blotchy color crept up his long gawky neck, across his cheeks.

"A man has been stabbed, Coleman, and you're the number-one suspect. It is in your own best interest to tell me the exact nature of your exchange with Quaide."

Coleman tensed for a moment, then the words flowed from his hand. *Told me to answer him. I tried. Sidestepped him—went below.*

"Miss Lucy apparently saw something."

Coleman stared at the paper, his tongue edging out the corner of his mouth. *If she said I stabbed him, she's lying!!!*

"No," Cap'n replied. "She witnessed the scene before the stabbing and came to me."

Coleman's face flushed a deep scarlet. Licked his lips and leaned toward the paper. *DON'T NEED A GIRL FIGHTING MY BATTLES!* The point of the pencil snapped, exploding the dot of the exclamation point into a smoky smudge.

Marni reached her hand out, rested it on his forearm. It was as though she willed him to meet her eyes. It was a different, deeper kind of seeing—the connection between her sea-green eyes and his gray-blue, transmitting something the cap'n and I could only sense. I knew the look, had felt its intensity when we'd first met back in Maine. The strain melted from Coleman's face, lines and creases relaxed.

"This man is telling the truth," Marni said, shifting her steady gaze to the cap'n. "He did not do the stabbing."

"How do you kn—" Cap'n began.

"I know. There are certain things I know, beyond any doubt."

The cap'n's eyes met mine. I nodded.

Cap'n Adams placed his elbows on the desk, rested his chin upon his folded hands. He studied Marni. Coleman. His eyes crept up the wall behind them, to the ceiling. Both index fingers popped up, crossing his lips. Finally, he exhaled loudly. "All right. But, given the seriousness of the offense, I'll need to question everyone aboard. *Somebody* stabbed him."

"Do what you must, of course," Marni said.

Cap'n nodded to Coleman. "You're free to go." Coleman did sort of an awkward half bow toward Marni, then he was gone.

Cap'n Adams leaned back in his chair, tipping the front legs from the ground. "So, who stabbed him? You must have an idea. Whoever did this will be put ashore when we arrive in the Azores. Replaced with someone we can trust."

I frowned, realizing Grady hadn't yet apprised the cap'n of our miraculous progress. There would be no stop in the Azores. Perhaps St. Helena.

"St. Helena, for sure," I said. The cap'n looked at me, his face a question. "It seems we strayed far off course," I said. "Grady can tell you—"

Marni interrupted. "Let's concentrate on the business at hand. Question all of them. I predict they will all be accounted for, at their stations and otherwise occupied, during the small window of time between when Lucy left them and arrived at your stateroom."

"What are you suggesting?"

Marni raised her eyebrows. "Nothing. We'll see what the investigation turns up."

She rose to leave, her hand on my shoulder. At the door she paused. "And Cap'n," she said, "I plan to have a talk with Quaide myself."

Outside in the corridor, I grabbed Marni's arm. "So, who do you think stabbed him?" I asked.

"I believe he stabbed himself."

My mouth dropped. "Why?"

"A game. A way to manipulate everyone aboard."

"What will you do?"

Marni stared down the narrow hallway as if gazing into the future. "He's leading us somewhere," she said, her voice hollow. She fingered the silver locket at her throat. "I've felt it from the moment I laid eyes on him. We're being drawn to where we need to be. Like it or not, I feel he's the one pointing the way—and I doubt he even recognizes his role in the whole of this. Perhaps it will make more sense once we discover what it is he's after. And how it is connected to our quest."

A chill swept along my back, down my arms. "I'm on watch. I need to go back."

"No worries, my dear," Marni said quietly. She took my hand and squeezed it, then headed to her stateroom.

I hurried toward the companionway, passing my cabin. There was something propped against the door. Something covered with a small piece of canvas. I knelt down and lifted the corner. I gasped.

It was octagonal, shimmering in shades of the palest pink, of lavender, and pearly cream. The tiny shells formed waves of blossoms in concentric circles. The sailor's valentine, completed! There was an *L* in the center, crafted with rows of tiny, swirled, bronze-colored snail shells.

I picked up the lovely plaque and beneath it was a scrap of paper, a note scrawled across it:

HAPPY BIRTHDAY L!
—W

17

"**L**and ho! Land ho!"

At the sound of Tonio's voice we all ran for the deck and lined up along the starboard side. I edged my way between Walter and Irish, casting sidelong glances Walter's way. For a moment our eyes met. His pinkie brushed mine, gripping the brass rail. I was filled with excitement! Walter beside me, and our little party that much closer to reaching Aunt Pru!

Tonio stood at the bow, spyglass in hand, pointing toward the island's volcanic peaks and ledges, just visible on the horizon. Cap'n shook his head.

"St. Helena," he said. "Impossible, but indeed, it is. Tonio—please."

Tonio passed him the scope, the cap'n took a perfunctory look and handed it back. "Indeed. James Bay. Will take us into port in Jamestown. A good week ahead of schedule, at least!"

"Ain't no doin' of ours," Grady said under his breath. "Ain't nothin' to brag about neither." He squinted in the hot sun, shading his eyes with his hand. Glared at Rasjohnny, then me.

Tonio wiped the sweat from his forehead. "St. Helena was good enough-a for Napoleon, it's good enough-a for me."

"He was a prisoner here." Walter looked at me, eyebrows raised. "Napoleon was. Exiled. We read about this island, remember?"

After all the days of silence, it felt awkward to be talking to him. But only for a second. "Yes," I said, remembering pouring over Father's log. "And the giant stairway—Jacob's Ladder. Almost seven hundred steps. Let's see if we can climb it!"

Georgie piped in, "Me too!"

Marni smiled. "It bodes well, despite Grady's worries," she said in a soft voice. "Ahead of schedule. Invisible hands ushering us on. We'll reprovision, stock the shelves for the sail around Good Hope. We can afford a few days' stay."

"Be good t' have a little solid ground b'neath me feet, it will!" Addie exclaimed. "Smell some island blooms!"

"And flowers you'll have, by golly," Cap'n quipped. And then, a little too quickly, "Flowers for *all* the ladies." He nodded toward Annie, who jumped up and down, hands clasped. But the twinkle in Addie's eye told me she knew Cap'n Obediah had been speaking mostly to her.

Quaide grumbled, "We can't stand here all day. We gotta bring 'er in. Take yer stations already!"

Since his stabbing, Quaide had been particularly ornery. Stalking around on deck, scanning the horizon. Fingers twitching. Especially since, just as Marni had predicted, everyone on board had been accounted for during the time of the stabbing—and thus, no one had been implicated. And besides this, like Grady, Quaide was perplexed and vexed about our ahead-of-schedule arrival.

"All hands!" Cap'n called heartily. "All hands!"

Closer and closer we came, carried by the southeasterly trade winds. The island's bare, rugged cliffs seemed to grow out of the azure seas. I grabbed Father's spyglass for a better look. A speck of white expanded into rows of whitewashed buildings huddled together in a narrow strip between the volcanic peaks. A bastion of stone created the walls of a fort, the long noses of cannons aiming out from the barricade.

Together we guided her in, bell tolling, announcing our arrival. Pugsley raised his snout skyward, picking up the tantalizing scents of land. We dropped anchor close to the rocky coast, and were met by a small clumsy steam vessel, its native crew waving wildly. "Taxi to shore!" they shouted. "We bring you in!"

"Batten down the hatches," Cap'n instructed. "Secure your valuables. We'll leave four men aboard ship at all times, weapons at the ready—a precaution. Irish. Tonio. Rasjohnny. Javan. You're first."

In a heartbeat Quaide was hauling himself over the side, scrambling down the ladder to the transport boat. Walter climbed with a squirming, wiggly Mr. Pugsley clamped tightly against his chest. "Be careful, Walter!" Annie cried. "Don't drop him!"

Georgie and Coleman were next, then the Reds, with Annie securely between them. Marni and I eased our way down amidst the oily smoke of the noisy vessel's dirty engine until we were standing on deck looking up at the bow of our ship. The figurehead of Uncle Victor and Aunt Margaret reached out over us toward the island, their wooden eyes staring blindly ahead.

The cap'n called Walter back and the two of

them ceremoniously helped Addie down. They no sooner reached us when Tonio drew the ladder back on board. The engine spit and coughed and we chugged to shore. I watched the *Lucy P. Simmons*, amazed, as always, by its stately beauty. At first I thought the movement behind it was a mirage—an optical illusion rising from the heat, the tides, from our extended time at sea. But no.

The transparent bowsprit, then the gracefully angled bow of the schooner wavered and rippled in the sun, edged out and around the *Lucy P. Simmons* until its entire ghostly silhouette shimmered like a shadow of light over our ship's starboard side.

I gasped and grabbed hold of Walter's and Marni's arms, one at each side of me. "Look!" I whispered.

Their gaze followed mine and I saw the vision of the phantom vessel reflected in their eyes. Together, we watched the specter ship sail ahead, hovering just above the surface of the water. Quaide stomped along the rail of the steamer, casting an occasional glance out to sea, with no reaction whatsoever.

Walter whispered, "He doesn't see it."

Marni agreed softly, "I don't know if he ever did. A certain kind of blindness, Quaide has." Our eyes flitted from Quaide to the ghostly ship and back. Nothing. In a moment, almost the entire mystery ship was visible, at least to us, moving sleekly and smoothly toward shore.

"Lookie there!"

I felt Grady's hot, sour breath in my ear, found him peering over my shoulder with his one good eye. "Oh, Mother of God," he rasped, blessing himself. "It's towin' another ship! Captured, no doubt. Doomed! Those sorry lads are doomed!"

Behind the phantom schooner a disabled square-rigged vessel limped along, riding low in the water, sails and masts at awkward angles. It was the black ship, the one I'd seen in Boston. The very same one the green-eyed man and our would-be kidnapper had boarded after greasing Quaide's hands full of money. I'd caught a glimpse of it on the horizon the morning of my birthday.

"Well, I'll be damned," Quaide mumbled. "They made it after all. And fast!" I spun around to see, first, a relaxing of his features, then a crease forming across his forehead. "How they're movin' is beyond me . . . crippled as she is. . . ."

"How's she *movin'*?" Grady laughed, a barking sound with no humor in it. "You don't see? The *Flyin' Dutchman* itself haulin' her in its wake!"

Quaide dismissed Grady with a wave of his beefy hand and exclaimed over the racket, "Shut up and cram your nonsense, Grady! *Flyin' Dutchman*?

Donkey dung! Seagull squat!"

Georgie piped in, "Porpoise poop!" Quaide and Georgie exchanged smirks.

"Georgie!" Walter admonished. "Enough!"

Grady pulled up his small wiry frame. The skin beneath his right eye twitched and a vein in his neck pulsed. He drew his fisted left hand back, forearm shaking. "I oughta . . . I oughta . . . make ya eat your own stinkin' little yella teeth, you big dumb ox. . . ." The steamship crew rushed forward, forming a ring around them, eyes glowing with excitement, hollering bloodthirsty encouragement.

"Don't hit 'im!" Georgie yelled, pushing his way between them. Walter grabbed his brother by the arm, as Grady threw a wild punch. Quaide simply leaned back, out of range, and spit out of the side of his mouth. Cap'n strode over, his angry words lost amidst the din of the engine. Much pointing of fingers, Pugsley now in the row, yipping and yapping.

All of this I observed with one eye, the other peeled to the specter ship towing the black brig, dropping her into a slip, continuing on a collision course with the pier. Marni and I held our breath, braced ourselves, and gasped as she lifted her prow at the last second, sailed right up over the land, and disappeared into a puff of vapor. At the same time we approached the dock, our steamship belching black smoke, her engine clanking, grinding, and snorting.

"That's the ship!" I shouted into Marni's ear. "The one from Boston! The one the mangy pirate and the man with the green eyes boarded—the guys who gave Quaide the money! Marni! Marni!" Why, I wondered, was the schooner assisting the pirate vessel?

Marni wasn't listening. Perhaps she was wondering the same thing. She fingered the silver locket at her throat, lips slightly parted, her sea-glass–green eyes fixed on the black ship, its deck now swarming with sailors. Finally, our Jamestown crew cut the engine and threw down the gangplank. Marni blinked and turned toward me, a vacant look on her face.

"Marni? Marni . . ."

Walter ran over, Georgie and Annie in tow. "Did you see that? There was almost a fight, but the cap'n broke it up." Annie stuck out her bottom lip. "I don't like that Quaide. He's just like Poppy!"

"Is not!" Georgie insisted.

"You don't have to worry," Walter said, giving each of their shoulders a squeeze. "I'm here, watching out for you. For both of you." Georgie squirmed from his brother's grasp. Walter sighed. Looked out to sea. "Where's the ship? The schooner?"

"Gone," Marni said softly. "For now, anyway. But we have company." She nodded toward the black square-rigger. "There are no coincidences."

An odd expression took hold of her features. A look of hope. Or controlled anxiety. She turned to me finally. "Something tells me that when we come ashore we'll need to be very, very careful."

18

We set off in small groups—Marni, Addie, and the cap'n to see to critical provisions, Walter, Georgie, Annie, and me off for a few hours of exploring. Pugsley trotted behind us, nose to the ground. "Stay together!" Marni had warned, "and meet back on board in three hours, tops." Georgie and I exchanged a glance. No need to remind us what kinds of things could happen in a seaport. It would be important to stay alert and aware of everyone's comings and goings. I watched Coleman and the Reds duck into a pub. Grady planted himself on the pier, arms crossed, leaning against a stone embankment, eyeing the black square-rigged ship suspiciously. As we walked I caught a glimpse of Quaide, who instantly disappeared into the maze of streets and back alleys.

I'd worried a bit about us standing out in this foreign place, attracting unwanted attention. But these quaint streets were filled with people from seemingly every land and tongue. It was easy to blend in. Welsh, Scots, and Brits, judging by their accents, and some who spoke something I judged to be Dutch. There were onyx-skinned Afrikaners, and men from unknown places in the Orient. I gave Annie's and Georgie's hands a tug. "Stop staring!" I whispered. "And no pointing! It's rude!"

"But . . . but," Annie protested, her eyes wide.

"Sh!" I admonished good-naturedly. It was hard, even for me, to refrain from gaping at the fascinating parade of humanity. Walter grinned at me over his siblings' heads and I felt instantly mature. Thirteen, for sure.

We trekked alongside a nearly dry moat surrounding the impressive stone gates of the city entrance. "Look at the castle!" Georgie cried, eyeing a tall archway on the left. "Do ya think we'll see a knight?"

"You never know," Walter said playfully. "Better pay attention. You don't want to get run over by a charging armored steed!" Annie grabbed my hand and inched a step closer. A warm feeling filled me. We were a little family. We would take care of one another. I looked at Walter. He nodded and blinked a silent assurance—and I knew he felt it too. And it was a relief to have Georgie looking up to Walter and out from under Quaide's thumb.

"There's Jake-o's Ladder!" Georgie yelled.

"Jacob's Ladder," I corrected. I was about to explain the bible story, but upon glimpsing the incredible tower of steps to our right, my voice deserted me. They were stacked almost straight up—literally more of a ladder than a staircase, extending as far as the eye could see.

"Oh my goodness!" Annie gasped.

"Ready?" Walter asked.

A shadow clouded his sister's face. "I don't know. . . . I . . ." Her bottom lip curled.

"Don't worry," Walter said. "If you get tired you can ride piggyback for a bit."

Georgie dashed ahead, counting each step as he went. "One, two, three, four . . ."

We followed, taking our time, waiting for Annie, who stepped up with her right, lifted her left to meet it, then repeated the process. At this rate it would take us forever to get to the top.

It wasn't long before we felt the heat of the sun

on our heads and shoulders, and our calves began to ache. Pugsley would scamper ahead, then plop down and wait for us, panting, tongue lolling. "Two hundred and seven . . . two hundred and eight . . ." At three hundred we sat and rested for a few minutes. Walter had been smart to bring a canteen of water, which we shared.

Onward and upward. Four hundred and eleven, four hundred and twelve . . . I climbed ahead, stopped, and turned. I was reminded of the first time I'd scaled the ratlines, my downward glance nearly causing me to swoon.

"Five hundred!" Georgie shouted triumphantly.

"Piggyback!" Annie whined.

"Okay," Walter said. "You two go ahead—we'll catch up to you."

Georgie and I started the final leg of our ascent. With maybe fifty steps left, he dashed ahead of me, wanting to be the first to reach the summit. I relished the bit of time alone, Georgie and Pugsley above me, and Walter and Annie below. I paused, braced myself against the stone foundation, and took my spyglass from my pocket.

To the left, the bright blue sea glittered, the pier a dark strip beside it. I scanned to the east and there was our ship. Javan was snoozing on the platform atop the mainmast, mouth agape, hands behind his head, elbows pointing outward. Ras-johnny and Tonio sat on the poop deck patching sails, and Irish washed down and swabbed the main deck.

Suddenly, just as it had in Boston, the scope reared to the right. Our ship, the pier, a row of white buildings flashed by, kaleidoscope-style. It scanned quickly back and forth, dizzying me on my steep stone perch, until it honed in on a narrow street near the entrance of town.

I was vaguely aware of Walter breathing heavily, approaching with Annie clinging to his back like a monkey. "We're getting close," he gasped. I could sense him sliding Annie down, until her dangling feet met the stairs, and she scrambled to catch up to Georgie. But I couldn't peel my eye from the scope.

"What is it?" Walter asked.

"I don't know . . ." I began, and then, there was Quaide striding along the pier. A movement farther down, from the gangplank of the black ship, caught my eye. I knew who would appear, even before I actually saw them—the nasty pirate with the red bandana and the green-eyed man who was carrying a canvas sack. Quaide waved for them to follow. Walter started to speak, but I quieted him with a raised index finger. Fascinated, I watched Quaide and the other two duck under an archway and carry on an intense conversation in the shadows. The scope pulled a bit more to the right, toward the type of gnarly, sprawling tree they call a black cabbage, native to the island. Its trunk grew right beside the stone foundation, shading the area near the wall where Quaide and his cohorts stood. The sunlight dappled through its branches, dancing on the ground around them. Quaide removed a watch from his pocket, squinted at it, then pointed at the *Lucy P. Simmons.* The other two nodded.

"Lucy, what do you see? Let me have a look."

"Hold on," I said, afraid to take my eye from the scope for even a second.

Something about the tree beside them continued to distract me. I moved the scope slightly, up and down along the silhouette of the black cabbage tree. Back and forth . . . wait! I squinted into the eyepiece. There . . . laid up against the trunk of the tree was another man. The sun glowing behind the tree cast the thin figure in shadow, so that the tree and his frame appeared nearly one. As Quaide gestured crudely to the pirate and the green-eyed man, both of whom nodded intently, the lanky fellow seemed to melt into the tree, his head tipped. He was eavesdropping—I was sure of it!

The suspicious trio continued their exchange,

unaware of the spy behind the tree. One by one, the green-eyed man pulled a variety of tools—picks and wrenches—from the canvas bag, as if explaining techniques for proper use. Quaide took each in his large hands, turning the implements this way and that, his mouth hanging slack as if sucking up the instructions. The pirate grinned, clearly enjoying the show-and-tell.

"Lucy?"

I was suddenly transported back to the stairway. Walter was standing so close I could almost feel the heat off his body. I slid the spyglass into my pocket and turned. Lost my footing. Gasped at the jolting sensation of almost falling.

Walter grabbed me. Spun me around and up, planting my feet firmly on the step above him. Our faces just inches apart. My mouth dropped open, heart racing. He shut his eyes, lazily, and closed the space between us. Staring at the beautiful fan of dark lashes against his skin, I experienced another wave of dizziness and took hold of him, certain I would topple backward.

Feeling Walter's breath, soft against my face, my own breathing stopped. His lips brushed mine, soft as velvet. I closed my eyes, and without willing it, my face tilted like a flower facing the sun.

Even before my eyes fluttered open I felt the

space between us turn airy and cool. He was already bounding up the remaining steps. "Come on," he called. "We need to catch up to them."

It was as if this gentle encounter never really happened. Had it just been my imagination?

I touched my fingers to my lips, clutched the railing, Quaide and his cohorts forgotten for an instant. By the time I glanced back toward the black cabbage tree, they were gone.

19

I stood, paralyzed, torn between following Walter up the steps and taunted by a vision of Quaide back on board, kneeling before the safe, poking around with his bag of tools. I peered down toward the water, trying to locate Quaide, then back over my shoulder. Walter was nearing the top of the stairs. Pugsley barked. "Walter!" I shouted. "We've got to get back!" The wind buffeted the sound and carried it off to sea. With Annie in tow, Walter continued his ascent, oblivious. *"Walter!"*

It was no use. I knew it wasn't safe to go alone, but what could I do? I only hoped that between the heat and the lure of the pubs Quaide might be waylaid on his return trek to the *Lucy P.* I raced downward.

At the bottom of the steps, heading into town, I became confused. The streets suddenly all looked alike. I ran one way, then doubled back, Pugsley beside me, nose to the ground. Traipsed down one narrow avenue that turned out to be a circle, ending up exactly where we'd begun. I stopped, short of breath. Sweating. Disheveled. Passersby stared. My heart raced and I felt something close to panic. I was alone, in a strange place that could be dangerous. The scar-faced pirate out and about. I frantically tried to recognize a landmark, a familiar corner, anything.

A hand on my shoulder. I gasped. Spun around.

It was Walter, panting, sweat beading across his forehead. Annie and Georgie, red faced and wide-eyed, one on each side of him.

"Where did you go?" he shouted. "What's wrong with you? We vowed to stick together and you run off by yourself?"

Annie started to cry. "Stop yelling," she begged. "You sound like Poppy!" Georgie's face went white. Walter flinched, knelt down, put his arms around them, and pulled them close. "I'm sorry," he whispered. "I was worried, was all." He stood, wiped the sweat from his face with the back of his hand, and looked at me over the tops of their heads.

"You left me on the steps," I said. After you kissed me, I thought. "I shouted for you—over and over! I have to get back." Fingers cupped, I whispered in his ear, "Quaide! The safe! I saw him through the spyglass!"

"What?"

"Just come on! Which way to the ship?"

"This way!" Walter led us, Pugsley yipping at our heels, and in no time we were back aboard the water taxi.

"I wanted to see the giant tortoise," Georgie complained.

"Me too," Annie whined. "It was up there at the top and then Walter made us leave!"

I inhaled and blew the air out through puffed cheeks. Leaning over the rail, Walter beside me, I stared straight out to sea. Quietly, so that Georgie wouldn't hear, I told Walter what I'd seen. By the time I finished explaining we were pulling up alongside our ship. Three blasts of the horn and Javan's face appeared above the starboard rail. He waved, and a moment later the rope ladder flopped over the side. We clamored up, first me, then the children, and Walter with Pugsley behind. I sent Annie and Georgie to the head to wash up, and to get a drink. They were both sweaty and covered in dust.

"Back early," Javan said, "and yous not de only ones."

"Quaide?"

Javan sauntered beside us across the deck, through the companionway. "Yup. Got 'ere five minutes ago."

"Hurry!" Walter and I started to run, Javan galloping to keep up.

"If yer somehow worried 'bout Quaide, you can stop worryin'." Javan grinned, his amber eyes twinkling. "Was in a big hurry—tripped. Took a header right here."

"What?" We'd just arrived at the chart room.

Javan pointed toward the stairwell. "Was like one of Quaide's ol' foots got tangled wid his other and over he went, whackin' his big dumb head in da wall! I seen it myself!"

"Where's Quaide now?" Walter asked.

"Rasjohnny take him to da galley ta dress da gash on 'is head."

"Javan, could you and Walter stay here and make sure no one goes into the chart room? I need a little time . . ."

"You got it, Miz Lucy. Me and Walter's up ta da task, right, Wally?"

Walter cringed at the nickname, but nodded.

I made my way to my cabin. I *had* to figure out the combination to the safe! Quaide may have been deterred for the moment, but, first opportunity, he'd be at it again. I couldn't risk him getting his hands on whatever might be in there that would help get me to Aunt Pru or solve the mystery of the curse!

I paused outside my room. A piece of paper had been left there, its slightly curled white corner just edging out underneath the door. I pushed it open, stepped in, and swept up the onionskin sheet.

It was a note, written in a familiar hand.

Miss Lucy,

I never did thank you for your speaking up on my behalf. Let this serve as a token of my gratitude, as one good turn deserves another.

I overheard Q onshore conversing with two men. Talk of busting into a safe that might hold secrets. Exchanging tools—shims, picks, and wrenches. Not sure if there's a safe aboard, but if so, you should know that there are others interested in its contents. I was going to inform Captain Adams—but I'm sure you can understand why I prefer to steer clear of Quaide and his doings. But, miss, perhaps you should speak to the cap'n. Whatever you do, be careful!

—Coleman

P.S. Also talk of finding a woman named Prudence? And retrieving a family treasure?

Of course! It was Coleman I'd seen, pressed against the black cabbage tree, eavesdropping on Quaide and his cronies! I understood the part about the safe—of course unscrupulous characters might be interested in whatever riches it might hold. But how in the world did they know about Aunt Pru? We'd never mentioned her. And what was this about retrieving a family treasure?

"Thank you, Coleman," I mouthed, as I stashed his note beneath my pillow. My flute buzzed in my pocket. Someow, the flute and the cards held the secret. I needed to discover the combination to the safe and, hopefully, the answers to many questions.

I grabbed my pad and pencil and climbed into the hammock, hoping my view of the sailor's valentine hanging on the far wall might calm my rattled nerves. As I put pencil to paper, the flute began to vibrate. "Ugh! Not now," I muttered. The vibration continued, increasing until it became a tone, and the tone continued until it became a tune—D–D–F, A–G–E, F–D–C, D. How could I concentrate?

As I pulled it roughly from my pocket, my fingers were sucked into place over the tone holes. "Stop!" I shouted, as the flute flew to my lips. I began playing in spite of myself—D–D–F, A–G–E, F–D–C, D. Over and over, like a mantra. I could barely catch my breath between bars. When I finally tore my lips away, the melody continued on its own. What was it trying to tell me?!

In seconds the incessant tune was accompanied by something like castanets. *Cl . . . cl . . . cl . . . clclclclclcl . . .* Sure enough, over on the shelf, the lid on the black box of cards jiggled. The top flipped off with a bang, and the cards danced out in a wave. On the final note, D, they shuffled themselves into three stacks.

I swung my feet to the floor and rushed to the shelf. The top card on each stack flipped upright and hovered, face first. The queen of spades, king of diamonds, and the bulldog-faced queen of diamonds. "Just the right *combination* of notes!" chortled the queen of spades. The three of them laughed, enjoying their private joke.

"Indeed, that's the *key*!" the dandy king added.

"*A lah-dee-dah-DEE!*" sang the queen of diamonds, in a strident vibrato.

"What are you trying to tell me?" I shouted. "What!"

"Tell you?" the beautiful, haughty queen of spades snapped. "We're not *telling* you anything! Figure it out for yourself!"

"Indeed!" the king exclaimed again, blowing his own card over, facedown.

"Only by fingering the correct combination

will you unlock the secrets," rasped the queen of diamonds. The king righted himself, nodding vigorously in agreement. The queen of spades bent forward from her card, turning toward the others, index finger to lips. "Shhhh! You fools! You've said too much already!" The force of her shushing blew both of them down, until they flopped and flapped themselves upright again. Then she pointed at me, her eyebrows raised in indignant arches. "That's it!" she said. "If you're as smart as they say, you can work it out!"

"As smart as who says? Who?" I persisted. But the life had already left them. Oh, how I longed to go to Marni, tell her about these vexing cards, and ask for her guidance. But the queen of spades' chilling warning held me back. I just couldn't risk the consequences, which were somehow tied to the curse. I had to solve this on my own!

My mother had said, *It's all in the cards, dear one.* I scooped up the three of them, fanned them in my hand. What had the two queens and the king said? I stared at them and their words came back to me: *Just the right **combination** of notes . . . Indeed that's the **key** . . .*

These were hints about the safe, of course . . . the combination, the key. . . . I studied the three mysterious initials beneath the queen of spades' portrait . . . MML . . . and an idea struck me. What if each letter had a corresponding number? On a scrap of paper I scrawled the alphabet. Counted . . . the letter *M* was 13. But if that was the first number in the series, the second was the same. It couldn't have two numbers repeated, one after the other, could it? What about the king? ES. *E* would be fifth, *S* was nineteenth. 5–19. Or, I thought excitedly, maybe 5–1–9. It was worth a try!

I ran toward the chart room, cards in hand. My fingers tingled in anticipation. Javan and Walter were sitting guard against the wall. I nodded as I burst past them, and shut the door behind me. Out of breath, I knelt before the safe.

To the right . . . 5 . . . Carefully, steadily, to the left back to 1. Then right to 9.

Nothing. I sat back on my heels. Exhaled in exasperation.

"Oh, come on!" I muttered. I pulled the cards from my pocket and glared at the three of them. The king puckered up and began to whistle. D–D–F, A–G–E, F–D–C, D!

The flute rose from my pocket, joining him in a maddening duet. It danced before me, tooling the tune, waving in front of the safe like a conductor's baton. It floated upward and, as it sustained the last note, whacked me on the head!

The queen of spades tipped back her lovely, sly face and laughed. The bulldog-faced queen *tsk, tsk*ed with her tongue, shaking her head. Her jowly cheeks wobbled. The king of diamonds shrugged, throwing both hands up as if to say, "Oh well . . ." And with that they were silent.

I snatched the hovering flute, caught it in mid-air, and shoved it, along with the cards, into my pocket, rubbed the small egg forming on my fore-head, and stomped back toward my cabin.

"Lucy?" Walter called after me.

"Just wait!" I said. "I'll be back!"

In my room I flung the flute on my bunk. It bounced and thunked against the wall. "What is it I just can't see?" I demanded. I sat on the floor and put my head in my hands. My hair fell forward, covering my face. I felt a tickle as the end of the flute nosed up sheepishly, delicately pushing aside my curls, sounding the D note ever so softly. I threw my head back, swiped at the hovering flute, and it—how should I say?—it flinched. I sighed. "All right," I murmured, feeling foolish speaking to a flute, "I'm sorry. Will you help me solve this mystery or not?"

Slowly, on the stream of that gently sounding low D, the instrument floated toward my book, *Fingering and Embouchure Technique for Flute and*

Recorder. It waved airily over the cover, blowing it open, the pages ruffling softly back and forth, back and forth. I watched as the yellowed sheets flipped, accompanied by that incessant D tone, until they lazily fluttered to a stop.

It was page one of the fingering charts, and there was the D—the round, open note hanging just below the staff. Beside it, the diagram of the six tone holes blackened.

But wait . . . beside it, the finger numbers were listed: 123/123, indicating that all three fingers of both hands should be covering the holes. I grabbed a pencil and paper and wrote out the fingering numbers without the slash—123123—six in all.

"What if . . ." I began, as I rewrote the sequence, adding a space between every two digits:

12–31–23? The flute shrilled an ear-piercing high note and then soared like a seabird, tootling the familiar tune, ornamented with trills and turns galore.

"That's it!" I tore the paper from the tablet, scooped up the flute, bolted from the cabin, and hurtled down the hallway. Javan and Walter looked up as I flew past into the chart room, yanking the door shut behind me. Knelt before the safe once again with sweaty hands. I paused, closed my eyes, and swallowed, sending a prayer to Mother, Father, to Aunt Pru. Please, please, let this work. Guide my hands. Open . . . please open!

Right . . . 12.

My mouth filled with a metallic taste. Gritted my teeth.

Left . . . slowly on to 31 . . . there . . .

I laid my fingers on the brass handle. It felt cool to the touch.

Carefully, carefully, right, steady on to . . .

23.

There was the slightest jolt as the knob slid luxuriously toward a soft but certain *CLICK*.

Like magic, the handle yielded, and the thick, heavy door swung slowly open.

20

On hands and knees, I leaned headlong into the cool, dark chamber. I swept my fingers across the shelf inside. Nothing!

Nothing?!

For a moment I sat back on my heels in disbelief. Had Quaide somehow beat me to it? I crawled forward until I was inside the safe, up to my shoulders. Walked my fingers deeper and groped around, slid my open palms across the smooth surface. Stretched, splayed, reached . . .

There—in the back right corner—I felt the accordion-folded edges of a cardboard folio leaning against the side wall. Seized it, and pulled it out. Tried to untie the cord wrapped around the middle that held the envelope-like flap in place. Anticipation made my fingers clumsy. As I fumbled, my heart began to race.

But wait. This wasn't a good idea, to open the folio here, the safe open and gaping, the door to the chart room unlocked. I thought of Coleman's note. I stood, clutching the precious booty protectively against my chest. Bent and gently pushed the thick armored door of the safe closed, spun the knob several times, and checked it. Locked solid.

I slipped out of the chart room, Walter and Javan still keeping watch. When Walter caught sight of the folio in my arms he broke into a grin. "I'll walk you to your cabin," he said.

"Need me to stay here, Miz Lucy?" Javan asked.

"No need," I said, anxious to get back.

"Looks like ya got what ya come for. Back ta work, den."

"Thank you, Javan!"

"Any time, Miz Lucy!" We waited as he scrambled off.

As soon as we were alone Walter turned to me. "You got it open! How did you do it, and what did you find?"

"Shh!" I said, patting the portfolio. "I didn't

open it yet!" We hurried toward my cabin. Just as I placed my hand on my cabin door Quaide burst through the companionway, a large white bandage on his forehead. My other hand, of its own accord, rose to my chest, instinctively protecting the folio.

Quaide stopped short, staring from the folio to the chart-room door and back. He chewed the inside of his cheek, glaring at us through hooded eyes. Then he slowly retraced his steps to the companionway, glancing back once, and disappeared.

Realizing I'd stopped breathing, I inhaled deeply. "Come on," I said. "No time to lose. Maybe you should keep watch." Walter nodded. "I'll be right outside." I slipped in and locked the door, just in case.

I dumped the contents of the folio on the bed, rifling through a stack of official-looking documents. Baltimore and Ohio Railroad, Union Pacific Railroad, Marconi's Wireless Telegraph Company, Cumberland Coal & Iron Company, Bath Iron Works, Britannia Mining and Smelting Company, Edison General Electric . . . most bearing the words *Certificate of Share—Capital Stock* and numbers on each—*one hundred shares, two hundred and fifty shares, three hundred and seventy-five shares . . .* Some indicated how much each share was worth—*One Hundred Dollars per Share* or *Sixty Dollars per*

Share. Stock certificates! I didn't know much about them, but I was sure they were worth a good deal of money.

This would be helpful, for sure, but I was disappointed. None of them provided any indication as to Aunt Pru's whereabouts or a single clue about the Simmons family curse.

At the back of the pile there was a large envelope, creased in the middle. I unfolded it and my heart nearly stopped. There was Father's name and our address back in Maine, scrolled in Aunt Pru's ornate hand. Quickly I withdrew the contents, sat down on my berth, and began to read.

> *Dear Edward,*
> *My research into our family's past and the mystery of the alleged curse continues to yield results! Now, I can well imagine you shaking your head, that famous smirk playing on your handsome face! Humor me if you must, but please, I beg you, read on. . . .*

I paused for a moment, remembering my aunt's face, stubborn, smart, and strong. I imagined her, pen in hand, earnestly scrolling this warning. And Father, setting it aside, not paying any heed. A flame of anger flickered in me. If he'd only listened . . . I shook my head and took a deep breath, trying to prepare myself for whatever else she had to say.

I have been to Ireland and have located the pub that once belonged to our grandmother, Molly O'Malley Simmons! It is a rough-and-tumble establishment, with a motley clientele. Some older folk still remember her and our grandfather, Edward the First, and let me say, upon inquiries about him, many an eyebrow was raised! They corroborated rumors I'd uncovered of his dubious reputation—his carrying-on the stuff of local legend.

I have learned that the grandfather we believed to be a much-respected sea captain was actually a privateer—hired by the government (and anyone else with the money to pay!) to hunt down pirates and other unsavory sorts who made an unlawful living at sea. He was, apparently, quite successful in these endeavors, until he began to skim off the top of the bounty, amassing great sums of money and treasure for himself.

Records prove that he did not flee Ireland from a criminal element seeking vengeance, as we had originally thought. No! He took flight to Australia as a fugitive, the law on his heels!

And, if this weren't enough, there's this: I have also discovered that, while married to

Grandmother, he had a liaison with a woman of questionable repute. A child was born to the two of them out of wedlock. Grandfather's getaway to Australia was, apparently, as much about distancing himself from this second family as it was about escaping his fate in Ireland.

I covered my mouth with my hand, then forced myself to read on:

After much red tape and many dead ends I have traced his steps across Australia, from Port Lincoln along what is now the Stuart Highway to his substantial landholdings near Alice Springs. I found his homestead—run-down, but habitable—tended by a caretaker who has welcomed me in. The deed had been transferred to our father, and is in my possession. An adjacent property—pasture land—is also deeded in the Simmons name. I am sending the deed to you, so that, upon seeing it, you might begin to believe that what I am telling you is true.

My plan is to fill in the missing pieces of our family tree—to discover who this woman was and what became of the child. With any luck, he or she might still be living, and this unlikely relative of ours might know something of the curse.

As always, be careful, Edward. I do not want you to continue the tragic legacy that Grandfather began, following him, and then our own father, to the depths of the sea. I will write as soon as I learn more.

Your loving sister,
Pru

Oh, Aunt Pru, I thought, you were *so* right! At that moment I felt such respect for her, such regret that her concern was disregarded. And a powerful love and admiration for her that nearly took my breath away. I fell back against my pillow, the stock certificates strewn about me. The information was shocking—my great-grandfather, who by all accounts had been a heroic figure in our family lore, was actually a thief? That the family fortune—perhaps even these valuable stocks—were bought with stolen money? I felt a flush creep up my neck and to my cheeks. My face burned. My great-grandfather—a cad and an outlaw?

I gathered up the stocks—dirty money, I thought, and slapped them into a pile. Slipped my aunt's prophetic letter back in its sleeve. But there, in the back of the envelope, was another paper, yellowed with age. I slid it out, anxious about what else I might find.

It was the deed to the property. One thousand acres, south of Alice Springs, Australia. There was our name, Simmons, across the bottom. The bit of good news in this was that the deed would serve as our compass—by locating this property we would discover the homestead where, hopefully, my aunt was still residing.

"Aunt Pru," I whispered, waving the deed. "Finally the clue that will lead me to you! Then we can solve this, together!"

The face cards in my pocket flipped up and out, landing in a row across my blanket. The queen of spades smiled wickedly. The king of diamonds shrugged. Cupping her mouth with a chubby hand, the queen of diamonds whispered conspiratorially, "You're getting warm. . . ."

"Warm?" I said. "No, I'm hot! Nothing can stop me now. Nothing!"

I took my stash, rolled back the Oriental carpet, and lifted a floorboard—the one that creaked every time I entered the room. Wrapped the folio in a piece of canvas, tied it securely, and tucked it out of sight.

21

The report of my findings spilled out as Walter and I headed toward the galley. There would be time for a steaming cup of java before Marni and Addie returned.

The galley was empty, the coffee perking merrily on the cast-iron stove. I got the mugs and Walter poured. Thick black brew, like oil, bubbled into the cups. "Cream and sugar?" I asked.

Walter nodded. "Can't drink the stuff plain."

I turned toward the counter where the fixings normally stood. "Hmmm," I said, "Rasjohnny must have stowed them away."

"Maybe over there," Walter said, pointing toward the shelves. We rummaged through this cabinet and that. Nothing. Maybe in the hinged chest near the corner. I knelt before it, threw back the lid. Pawed through bags of flour and cornmeal, salt, rice . . . pinched several black-shelled weevils disturbed by my searching. Felt a smaller parcel beneath all these. Grabbed and pulled, the back of my mouth filling with saliva just thinking about the sweet, brown granules.

But what emerged was not a bag of sugar.

"Got it?" Walter asked, carrying the two mugs. Then he froze, staring over my shoulder. "What's that?"

We gaped at the stuffed effigy in my hand. A thick torso, sausage arms, a bulbous head. Grains of rice glued on created a pair of blank eyes. Felted fabric gathered tightly created the look of two generous lips, the bottom one protruding insolently. Even without the blotch of red on the right shoulder where the pin was stuck, and the ankles tied together with twine, anyone could see it was Quaide. I held it for a moment before I dropped it back in the chest. My heart was racing.

Footsteps behind us. Walter spun around, the coffee sloshing over the rims of the mugs.

"Rasjohnny!" I exclaimed. My voice sounded

strange to me, thin, airy. He stared at us, blinked, glanced up at the ceiling and back.

"You's needin' somethin' you can't find," he said softly. "And you's findin' somethin' you wasn't lookin' for, dat right?"

"That's for sure," Walter said.

I held up the voodoo doll. "Quaide."

Rasjohnny chewed his bottom lip. Nodded. I thought of how Marni had sensed that Quaide had stabbed himself and how he'd inexplicably tripped over his own two feet outside the chart room.

"So, this is how he got *stabbed*? And how he fell and whacked his head?"

"Voodoo only work when da spirit's open. If he didn' have no evil in 'im, da magic most likely wouldn't touch 'im. But he's evil, yes he is. So's dis offers pr'tection fer da rest. We's talked 'bout magic before. Ain't no power in it, less da spirit's open. Like joins wid like."

Walter shook his head. "You're saying you caused all this? Quaide getting stabbed, then tripping in the hall . . ."

"No! I's not sayin' dat. I's sayin' dat Quaide, he invite evil on hisself. And me—I's only led by da magic I be feelin' 'board dis ship. Pow'ful magic it is! You know dat, ain't dat right?"

Walter and I exchanged a glance. Powerful,

indeed. We left without a sip of java or an ounce of peace of mind. It was time for another family meeting, that was for sure. We headed up top to watch for Marni and Addie. In fact, the water taxi had just pulled up, and Javan was lowering the ladder.

"Let's meet in Marni's stateroom," I said. "I'll go ahead." I needed a few minutes to gather my thoughts.

Halfway down the stairs I stopped short. I heard two voices—and one of them was Quaide's. I snuck to the door and inched it open just a crack. Placed my ear against the opening.

"Come 'ere, mate," Quaide drawled. "I 'ave an important mission for ya—if you're man enough fer the job." Peeking through the space I watched Quaide give Georgie's shoulder a quick squeeze and squat down in front of him so they were nearly eye to eye.

Georgie nodded eagerly. "Whatever it is, I can do it."

Quaide bit his bottom lip. "I'd like t' think so, but yer still a little young. Ya see, sometimes a sailor has to do stuff that ain't easy. Stuff others aboard might not understand at first. So he's gotta be tough. Determined. Gotta be able to keep a secret."

"I can do it!" Georgie repeated.

Quaide made a show of looking pensive,

forehead creased, lips pursed. He rubbed his chin as though deep in thought.

"I'm not too sure you're up to it. Javan's older. He could do it, fer sure."

I felt my blood boil. He was baiting Georgie, suckering him in to something. And Georgie was taking the bait, hook, line, and sinker. I thought of bursting through the doorway and putting an end to this charade, but I held back.

"No, Quaide," Georgie begged. "Don't ask Javan! Please! You'll see, I can do it. Whatever it is . . ."

"Hmmmm . . . I dunno . . ."

It took everything I had not to jump out and shake some sense into Georgie. But not before I found out what Quaide was up to.

"See, a real sailor sometimes has to steel hisself against family 'n' friends. Y'know—in order to do what needs doin' without interference. Blatherin' to this one and that, like ya might at home—that don't cut it at sea. Which is why *real* sailors leave all that onshore . . ."

"You can trust me, Quaide. *Please*. I won't tell Walter or Annie, or . . ."

"Lucy. Ya can't tell her neither. 'Specially her. Or the old lady. I could trust Javan t' keep his piehole shut."

"I won't tell, I swear!"

"I might try ya out—but *one* word, *one* wrong move . . ."

"Don't worry!" Georgie made a twisting motion in front of his lips, as though turning an invisible key. "Locked!" he promised.

"Awright," Quaide said. "Here ya go." He lowered his voice. I strained to catch each word. "I seen Coleman up to some funny business. Ya know how quiet and sneaky he is? Never wantin' to attract any attention? Well, now I know why! I seen 'im fiddlin' with the safe in the chart room. Spied him poppin' the lock like a pro, and makin' off with a pile of papers. Closed the safe back up with nobody but me the wiser."

"Oh no!" Georgie exclaimed.

"We gotta trap 'im, so's to prove his guilt."

"But how?"

"I seen him sneak into yer sister and Lucy's cabin with the stash and come out without it. He's a sly one. Musta hid it right under their noses. So, what you need to do is get in there and dig around till ya find it. Then, ya give it me and I'll turn it in to the cap'n."

"Why don't we just tell Marni and the cap'n right now?"

Quaide stood up. I held my breath, praying he

wouldn't see me through the crack in the door.

"Look, never mind. Ferget it! Here I was gonna set ya up to be the hero in all this, and instead you wanna go runnin' off cryin.'"

"No! No! I *do* wanna be a hero!"

"Then get to it—but be careful! Yer lookin' fer a pile of papers. Or, a small brown folder. Don't let neither of 'em catch ya, ya hear me? It'll be our secret till we get ta 'Stralia. Then, we'll turn the crook in!"

"I got it!"

"Here," Quaide said. "Take this." He thrust forward a canvas sack. "Shove it all in there. And when ya got it, here's our secret signal. Can ya whistle?"

"Uh-huh."

"Three short blasts and one long, like this . . ." He puckered up and blew through his teeth: "*Phweet-phweet-phweet-wheeeeeee!* You try it."

"*Phweet-phweet-phweet-wheeeeeee!*"

"Good enough. Repeat it till ya hear me answer. Then we'll meet below, next-a the bilge pump. Got it?"

"Got it!"

"Now go!"

Never in my life had I felt such rage! It took every ounce of resolve not to immediately confront him. Somehow I managed to wait until I was certain they were gone, then I rushed to my cabin. Closed the door behind me with a trembling hand. A steely resolve rose up inside me. I would somehow outsmart him, trap him. And to think that if I hadn't overheard him he might have gotten away with it! I knelt, lifted the floorboard, removed the pile of stocks and documents. Where should I put them?

Just then I heard Addie and Annie in the corridor. Addie! Of course!

The door opened and Annie bounded in. Hugging my parcel to my chest with one hand, I grabbed my flannel nightshirt hanging on the peg, headed Addie off in the doorway.

"Addie . . . can you do something for me? It's important."

"Course I can, ye know that now, don't ye? What 'tis it, lass?"

"Take these papers—they're important, and Quaide is trying to get his paws on them."

She eyed me closely. "Are you all right then? You've a strange look in yer eye, is all."

"I'm just determined," I replied. "And anxious."

Addie shook her head. "He's no good, that Quaide. No good atall. Whyn't I just tell Cap'n? Obediah'll lock the cuss down below fer the remainder of the voyage and be done with 'im!"

"No! There's something I need to do first. Trust me."

Addie bit her lip and frowned. "Nothin' to put ye in harm's way? I won't be party t' that, y'know!"

"No," I lied. "Of course not."

"Then what 'tis it ye need me t'do?"

"Take these papers, and somehow stitch them to the inside of this nightshirt. Use a dish towel or something to make a big pocket. So that if you saw the nightshirt folded in a drawer nobody'd be the wiser. See what I mean?"

"Ah," she said, nodding her head, warming to the task. "To make a hidin' spot no one'd suspect. Easy 'nough." She handed me her shawl. Lowered her voice and glanced about. "Quick now, wrap 'em in 'ere."

We folded the shawl around my precious papers and Addie clasped it against her body, the fringed edges falling naturally over her arm. Over her other arm hung my nightshirt. She leaned toward me.

"Soon as the sewin's finished, I'll fold the nightshirt and tuck it safe in the drawer alongside me bloomers." She winked, and a wave of feeling welled up in me.

"Love you, Addie!" I blurted, throwing my arms around her. She hugged me tight, my precious papers pressed between us. After a moment she stepped back.

"Oh, child," she said, her eyes twinkling with tears, "I love ye too, I do! Always 'n' forever!"

"And Addie—as soon as you're done, come to Marni's stateroom. And bring the cap'n."

22

There was no time to waste, as I didn't want Quaide to have another opportunity to manipulate Georgie, or for Georgie to be wracked with worry over the task he'd been duped into performing. Soon after sailing out of St. Helena, on the way south toward the Cape of Good Hope, I carried out my plan. Addie kept Georgie and Annie amused in the stateroom, out of earshot. Grady, Coleman, Rasjohnny, and Javan sailed the ship. Smooth seas and sunny skies.

My heart raced as I stood at the hatchway, lantern and folio in hand. To muster up some courage,

I thought about Aunt Pru, and my determination doubled. I took a deep breath, puckered up, and whistled. *Phweet-phweet-phweet-wheeeeeee! Phweet-phweet-phweet-wheeeeeee!*

I waited. Whistled again. *Phweet-phweet-phweet-wheeeeeee!*

And then, the response. *Phweet-phweet-phweet-wheeeeeee!*

I threw back the hatch and felt for the ladder with my foot. Struck a match and lit the lantern. Clinging to the lamp handle, folio pressed against my chest, I crept down into the shadows. I pulled the hatch closed, shone the lantern this way and that, trying to get my bearings.

I nodded. Everything was exactly as planned. Still, my heart thumped wildly. I inched toward the bilge pump, and hid behind some crates. The water sloshed below, its foul smell filling my nostrils. Something skittered over my foot, and I stifled a scream. Two small glowing eyes stared at me through the dank darkness. A rat! I kicked at it with my boot, trying to frighten it away. It curled back its mouth and hissed, revealing a row of small pointed white teeth. I slapped the portfolio against my hand to frighten off the aggressive rodent. It recoiled and disappeared between the planking, leaving me unnerved and jittery. "Get a hold of yourself!" I whispered. And not a moment too soon! There was a *whack* as the hatchway door was flung back, and the thudding of Quaide's boots on the ladder. I peered into the inky gloom, trying to gauge his progress, praying nothing would go wrong.

"Well, where are ya, Georgie m' boy? No need to be hidin'! Nobody here but yer ol' buddy Quaide!"

I struck a match, relit the lantern, and stepped into the small circle of light. "Georgie isn't here!" I hissed. I waved the folio in front of him. "Is this what you're after?"

Quaide blinked, once, twice. Then he narrowed his eyes. "That little cuss spilled the beans, didn't he?"

"No, he didn't. The fact is, I overheard your entire conversation with him. And I wasn't going to let you set him up. Trying to trick a little boy into doing your dirty work! Stealing from me! I know what you want—I just haven't figured out why."

"You can't prove nothin'," Quaide said. "It's yer word against mine."

He sprang forward, grabbed the folio from my hands. Opened it. "It's empty!" he shouted. Nostrils flaring, he flung it into the bilge. It hit the water with a splash. He lunged toward me. I jumped back, nearly losing my balance, teetering for a moment at the edge of the precipice. "Lucky ya didn't fall in," he snarled, clasping and unclasping his hands, inching closer and closer. Through clenched teeth he muttered, "I oughta . . ."

"Oughta what?" said a deep voice.

Quaide spun around. The cap'n stepped out of the darkness, pistol drawn, the Reds, Irish, and Tonio behind him. Marni and Walter, arms folded, across from them.

Quaide turned in one direction, then the other.

"Give it up," the cap'n growled. "There's no way to escape."

"She set me up," Quaide roared. "I didn't do nothin'!"

"You can tell it to the law when we reach Australia," the cap'n said. "Stealing is a crime—and involving a little boy in it . . ."

"I heard they got the largest penal system in the world there," Irish quipped.

With the cap'n's pistol aimed at Quaide's chest, Tonio and Irish wrenched one thick arm then the other behind Quaide's back, while the Reds slapped on the manacles. Then they led him to the brig—a small barred-off area where he'd spend the rest of this voyage.

Marni, Walter, and I watched as the crew dragged the hulking figure off. My knees were weak, and my hands shook. I should have felt relieved, but when Marni and I exchanged glances I saw my mixed feelings reflected in her eyes.

"We're safe for now, I suppose," I said. "But there'll be Georgie to contend with, and the bigger question—is it just greed driving Quaide? Or something more?"

Marni shook her head. "If it was only monetary gain he was after, I'm not sure he would have signed on with us in the first place. Why wouldn't he have just sailed with his mates aboard the black ship, pursuing more lucrative targets? No—Quaide is somehow a part of this quest."

At that moment the ship dipped and bobbed as if affirming her words. We exchanged glances and Marni went on. "I can't imagine a pair of handcuffs and a stint in the brig is going to change Quaide's agenda. We'll see what Australia brings. . . . He might decide to talk when faced with the prospect of arrest—but I doubt it."

Walter nodded. Sighed deeply. "Speaking of talking—I have to go and find my brother."

23

"Entering the roaring forties!" Cap'n exclaimed, both hands on the ship's wheel, hair blowing straight back off his face. We were under full sail, speeding forward at over ten knots. "I plan on taking full advantage, to continue to move us along ahead of schedule." I pulled my cloak around me tighter. Every day seemed a little colder than the last.

Marni nodded, turning toward Walter, Georgie, and me, all of us wide-eyed. "The 'roaring forties'—a phenomenon that occurs after crossing the equator, heading toward the South Pole. Hot air rising, cooler air dropping—produces strong winds like nowhere else on the planet."

"The furious fifties—even better!" Irish piped in, flashing his wide white smile. "Drop south to fifty degrees, or, if you're feelin' lucky, to the shriekin' sixties! Woooo hoooo! We'll fly like the wind!" He raised a fist in the air, his eyes wild.

"So full of big-headed idears and Irish bravado," Grady muttered. "Ever actually sail the fifties and sixties? Bergs! Ya gotta be on constant watch for the bergs. Hit a big chunk of floatin' ice and you're done fer! Need a lookout in the crow's nest ever minute—alert, vigilant! And cold? You never felt cold like ya do below forty degrees latitude—drop to the fifties and sixties and it's colder than a belly blue hell!" The Reds snickered and Grady cast them a withering glance. "And lemme remind you pair of fools that it ain't fer nothin' that the cape was first named Cape o' Storms. That southwestern tip of Africa—a ship's graveyard!" He counted off the wrecks on his gnarly fingers. "There was the *Joanna*, the *Arniston*, the HMS *Guardian*, the HMS *Sceptre*. . . ."

"Always belly-achin'!" Irish replied good-naturedly, dismissing Grady's concerns with a wave of his hand. "And I suppose we should be worryin' about the *Flyin' Dutchman* out here, too!" The others laughed, a little nervously, it seemed to me.

"Matter o' fact," Grady snarled, "this is just where it all started—Cap'n Vanderdecken makin' his deal with the devil—sold 'is soul for speedy passage round the cape. Hit a storm and the fool pressed on—damned himself and 'is crew to sail the seven seas for all eternity aboard their ghostly ship. Laugh if ya want, but I seen things through the years . . . but never as much as I seen on *this* voyage. . . ."

"Gentleman!" The cap'n silenced them with a stern look. "I believe we're all aware of the inherent challenges. Great care will be taken, and we will not sacrifice safety for speed."

As if on cue, a blast of frosty air bore down on us, whipping my hair across my eyes, stinging my forehead. The ship nosed sharply up, then down, riding a wave crashing against the bow. A frigid sheet of water exploded over the rail and slapped the timbers, its icy spray christening us for the next leg of our journey. "Here we go!" Irish yelled.

"Put on your woollies," Cap'n advised, "oilskins over. Hats and hoods. Boots. Rasjohnny'll keep the java brewing. And batten down your hatches. Rough seas ahead, for sure."

I glanced at Marni, staring at the horizon. Under gray skies and against steely seas, her eyes appeared a moody shade of cyan blue. Lips slightly parted, fingers twisting the locket at her throat, a faraway look shadowed her face. It was an expression I'd come to know, part of the mystery of her. It made me anxious. What was it that sometimes stole her attention, taking her far from us?

"Come on," Walter said, tapping my shoulder. "Better go change. Georgie, you too. Bundle up!"

I nodded, acutely aware of the spot he'd poked near my collarbone. It had taken some doing, but I'd managed to switch my watch with Coleman, in order to be on duty the same time as Walter. As we left I stole a look back at Marni, her rapt attention still focused out to sea, a light snow swirling about her. I paused, and took out my spyglass, aiming it in the direction of her gaze.

"Marni," I whispered, peering through the eyepiece. "Sometimes I wonder . . ." I stopped. My words trailed off. She didn't seem to hear. There, in the distance, I saw it, its silhouette unmistakable. The black ship, the one carrying the pirate and the green-eyed man. Always a presence just behind us. Perhaps Marni was worrying about that as well.

"What is it?" Walter asked.

I shook my head. "Just that ship—the black square-rigger. It's following us."

"Let them try," Walter said, grinning. "There

isn't a ship around that can keep up with the *Lucy P. Simmons*! And the farther south we go, the better time we'll make!"

We dashed below, the ship pitching dramatically, and ran to our respective cabins. I closed the door snugly behind me and my eyes adjusted to the dim light. Annie lay, sprawled stomach-down on the floor, the cards spread around her. Ida stood behind her mistress, one of the hens perched on her back.

"Lucy," she called, "the backs of these cards? Every one of them is different! Look!"

I squatted beside her and watched her sort the cards into groups. I'd been aware that the backs of the cards were decorated with busy, complicated panoramas, but my fascination with the face cards had overridden any interest in what was depicted on the backs. I picked one up to look more closely. It was covered in tiny elaborate pen-and-ink line drawings, the figures and scenes surrounded by intricate scrolls and curlicues, so that every smidgen of space was filled.

"See, these are all of stuff at sea," Annie instructed, pointing to one group. I studied them, picking up this one and that, and yes, these cards were illustrated with tiny ships and crews, whales, pirates—all the stuff of seafaring.

"And here—these ones are all places on land." She jabbed a small finger toward another bunch of cards. I detected a seaport, buildings, a town scene. And, upon careful examination, it was apparent that each card was unique, the small stick-like people situated differently, scene to scene. One of a kind—every card was one of a kind.

A repetitive mushy sound made us both look up. Ida's jaw was moving, her long pink-gray tongue swiping her muzzle. To our horror we watched the edge of a card disappear into her mouth.

"Ida! No!" Annie screamed, jumping up. The frightened hen flapped her wings and flew to Annie's bunk in a small cloud of feathers. Ida, unimpressed, swallowed languidly, the lump that was one of our cards traveling down her throat.

"Annie!" I shouted. "You have to take better care of the cards! And get her out of here! She's a menace!" My knees felt weak. I'd somehow been entrusted with the cards and now one was gone.

"Baaaaaaa," Ida bleated, as if to say, "Too bad!" Thank goodness I'd removed the king and queen of diamonds and the queen of spades from the deck and hidden them safely away. I couldn't imagine what would have happened if Ida had swallowed one of them. I doubt they would have gone down as easily. "Out!" I yelled, pushing open the door.

The stubborn creature started out just as the ship reeled forward and back at a steep angle, sending her sprawling. That's what you get, I thought.

"Annie, pull out your woollies and get in your bunk," I said. "Hunker down! Rough seas ahead! But gather up those cards first!"

She did as she was told. I tucked my flute and the face cards in beside the box and soundly replaced the board.

By the time I left the cabin, moving slowly in multiple layers of woollies and oilcloth, the ship was rocking and rolling. A perpetual crash, splash, and roar served as accompaniment, the music of the waves battering the hull.

Passing through to the companionway was nearly impossible with the strength of the oncoming gale blowing in. I shouldered the wooden panel, threw my weight against it, managed to crack it but a smidgen. The wind shrieked through the space, mocking me. I wondered how Quaide was faring down below, chained in the brig—and if Georgie was wondering as well. He'd taken the news of Quaide's betrayal hard, but was finally coming around a bit. I also worried about traversing the most difficult part of our voyage minus one sailor. Suddenly another pair of palms pressed against the wood, another shoulder beside mine. Heave ho!

Walter and I pushed until the door slammed back against the wall and we barreled through.

All hands on deck, oil-skinned figures manning lines and sails as the ship rose and plummeted on twenty-foot swells. I looked up and saw what appeared to be a huge raven perched atop the crow's nest, peaked oilskin hood pointing to sea like a beak, wide canvas sleeves flapping like wings. It was Tonio, on the lookout for icebergs.

I grabbed hold of the ratline and started to climb. No one had more at stake than I—if there were bergs to be spotted, I'd spot them. The higher I got, the fiercer the wind, lashing around my limbs, trying to suck me from the lines. Snow squalls blustered in howling spirals. The enormous height of the waves pitched the ship forward and back at extreme angles. Scaling the mast was like climbing the back of a giant rocking chair, one minute slanting out over the seething steely sea, the next swinging past nothing but sky.

Up, up I went until I felt the edge of the platform and grabbed hold with one hand, the other grasping about, blindly trying to get Tonio's attention.

In an instant I felt his iron grip on my arm, then on the other, and he drew me up.

"You?" he shouted. "*Lei è matta!* You crazy!" He

shook his head, incredulous. The hood of his cloak and his drooping mustache were both dripping icicles, giving him the look of a shrouded walrus.

I hunkered down beside him, tethering myself to the mast with the end of a flapping line. "Bergs!" I shouted, pointing from my eyes to the horizon. He nodded, training his gaze back to the sea. I took out my spyglass, peered into the eyepiece.

"*Guarda!*" he exclaimed. "Look!" He pointed to an area of sea off the starboard side where a whole school of ice chunks bobbed and churned. Each was the size of a large boulder. Steam rose off the water around them. "Growlers," Tonio said through gritted teeth. He took up a small dented brass bugle, put it to his lips, and blew three short blasts. In an instant the ship veered left. "You-a never wanna sail downwind of a berg," he yelled. "Where there's growlers—there's-a berg. Berg is-a the mamma, growlers is-a the *bambini*—the babies. Both can put a hole in-a the ship!" All this he said without his eyes ever leaving the horizon. A chill rattled through me, clear to the bone. Bergs. Growlers. Shipwrecks.

I took my spyglass again and trained it off the starboard side, where the field of growlers curtsied in the waves. Slowly, back and forth, I swept the lens. There, off to the west, a huge mountain of ice appeared between the crest of the waves.

"Berg!" I yelled, poking Tonio and pointing. "Berg!"

He turned his hawk eyes westward. "Not-a whole berg," he shouted. "A bergy-bit!" Again, three blasts of the horn. He gestured, palms a foot or so apart. "Bergy-bit, this-a big." He stretched his arms as wide as they'd reach. "Ice-a-berg, this-a big! *Capisce*?"

The two of us fell silent—it was nearly impossible to hear, the wind roaring like a freight train. We must have been flying at almost twelve knots. Faster than I'd ever sailed. The only thing warm was our own breath, evident before us in small vaporous puffs that blew back and froze on our faces.

"Off portside!" I bellowed. "Portside!" I pointed furiously to the left, jabbing Tonio with my elbow. Like a pointed, snow-covered mountain peak, the top of an iceberg appeared behind a wall of steam and whirling snow. Tonio's eyes grew huge. Put his bugle to his lips, puffed out his cheeks, and blew one long blast followed by two short, urgent ones. He struggled to his feet, grasping the mast with one hand, sounding the alarm again as he scanned starboard.

We spotted it at the same instant—out of

nowhere—the black ship, hurtling over the waves, changing course before our eyes. Clearly, they'd spotted the berg as well and, desperate to avoid it, were bearing down, their bowsprit aiming at us like a knight's pike, ready to plunge a hole in our prow.

Another burst of Tonio's horn, but even I could see that no matter which way we turned we were doomed. Off the starboard side the steam swirled into thinner wisps of mist, revealing glimpses of the silhouette of the huge triangular iceberg. By the sudden wild scrambling below, we knew our mates had seen it too. There was nothing to be gained by us staying aloft. If we were going down I wanted to be with Marni and Addie, with Walter, Georgie, and Annie.

I scrambled down the ratlines, swinging and bobbing, frantically grasping with numb, aching fingers. A glance in either direction affirmed my worst fears. Iceberg portside, and pirate ship starboard, the *Lucy P. Simmons* between them.

I jumped the last six feet to the deck. Sprawled across the glass-like surface slick with ice. It all appeared as in a dream—Marni with Georgie in tow, words I couldn't hear pouring from her lips, Walter and the Reds desperately working the thick lines, Addie holding Annie, her face melting in relief when she saw me, the cap'n, Coleman, and Irish—six hands to the wheel—but which way to turn? Rasjohnny and Javan, running the winch, lifeboats poised to drop, tipping them beside the rail. Yanking life preservers out the poop cabin, aft. Pugsley, near the companionway, crouched on shivering haunches. Georgie gesturing wildly at the black ship. All futile.

Driven by the screaming wind, the unforgiving sea churned up taller, angrier waves, rollers and combers both. The *Lucy P. Simmons* charged up over the backs of them, some thirty feet or more, crashed down as they peaked and broke. The vicious gusts drove furious upsurges from all directions, hitting us starboard, then port, throwing us perilously side to side. We were soaked clear through our oilskins, exhausted from convulsive shivering, our faces red and raw from the salt and the cold. All of our sails, ripped and slashed into streamers, whipped about like a hundred flags of surrender. There was nothing we could do in the face of it but hold on. As if pulled by some invisible force, Addie and Marni, Walter, Georgie, Annie, and I drew together, encased in one another's arms. Pugsley too, slipping and skidding across the deck, nosed into the middle of our group and huddled at our feet. With frozen hands we clung to the mast and to one another, so as not to get swept, one by one, into the frigid sea. No—together—this is how we'd go down.

Suddenly, the black ship appeared directly before us, hurtling over the top of a thirty-foot swell. Up, up it soared, its bowsprit aiming straight toward the sky. The wave crested and the black ship plummeted, the underside of its hull looming over our bow. There was a huge rush of air, a deafening crash, a bone-shuddering jolt. The crack of timbers splitting, the pitiful creak and moan of our ship coming undone, the prow of the black ship splintered and agape, her ruin mingled with our own. A torrent of raging water gushed across the deck carrying shattered pieces of our ship, and with it, our hope.

24

The *Lucy P. Simmons* lurched forward, the fractured black ship attached to us like a wounded appendage. Men crawled from the wreck of the square-rigger onto what was left of our deck, stunned. Others jumped into the icy sea, like water rats, to certain death.

Cap'n shouted frantic orders, his arms still straining at the wheel. Half his words were lost in the pandemonium. "We're takin' on water too fast! You two—Reds—pump the bilge! Irish—men overboard! Try and scoop 'em up in the net!" The men stumbled about like zombies, sloshing through the frigid water, attempting to follow orders, but too numb and overwhelmed to see them through. "Tonio! Coleman! Bail! Get them all to bail! Smack Grady out of his trance! Where the devil are the Reds? All hands! All hands!"

Desperately, we waded through the freezing cascade of sea lapping the deck, trying somehow to save what we could and clear away the rest. Chaos. Utter chaos.

Then, like a beast crawling out of its den, I saw Quaide emerging from a pile of fractured timbers, manacles still encircling one wrist. He thrust the wreckage this way and that, crashing over and through it. Eyes wild, he half ran, half splashed his way toward the cavernous hole in the hull of the black ship.

I screamed for Walter, or Coleman, anyone who could stop him, but my voice was completely lost in the wind. I watched Quaide dive into the opening and disappear, as though swallowed up by a great black monster. In response, the *Lucy P. Simmons* seemed to let out a roar. It shimmied and lurched. My heart fell. He'd escaped—if you could call throwing yourself into the bowels of a sinking ship an escape.

I turned back toward Walter, who, along with Rasjohnny and Javan, was throwing anything of value up onto the poop deck. But they were no match for the water and the pitching of the ship, which swept most of it off again. Addie beside the cap'n, her hands next to his on the wheel. Only Marni stood quietly, still as stone, eyes fixed on the black ship.

Somehow the waves carried the two damaged vessels forward, and our disabled prow cut through the mist surrounding the iceberg. I was aware of Annie yanking me by the arm, trying to drag me toward the lifeboats. But every fiber in my being refused to move. My feet stayed planted, a current of icy water surging around them. Marni, too, remained beside me, her eyes sweeping from the wreck of the black ship to the iceberg and back. Walter grabbed me around the waist and lifted me toward the lifeboats. I kicked and thrashed until he put me down, my eyes never leaving the mist-shrouded berg. It took several more moments before I realized that we were no longer moving under our own power—and yet we were not sinking. I squinted as our forward progress parted the low-lying cloud.

As the vapor cleared, they saw it too. Pugsley threw back his head and howled.

What we'd assumed was the peak of the iceberg was actually the tip of a ghostly snow-white sail; the large triangular shape we'd supposed was the mountain of ice was really the silhouette of the phantom vessel.

Grady stood alone. His deathly pale face and ogling eyes a mask of terror. He shrieked, "The *Dutchman*! The *Flying Dutchman*!" Dropped to his knees, still screaming, the veins and muscles in his neck straining like ropes on a winch. "Thou, O Lord, that stillest the raging of the sea, hear, hear us, and save us, that we perish not! We beseech thee, Lord, have mercy upon us!"

Everyone froze and turned toward the phantom ship, finally visible to everyone aboard. It seemed to glow, a powerful bright white light emanating from its sails. The sky directly around it suddenly lit by a halo of otherworldly radiance. It transformed our faces in stark contrasts of light and shadow. The glittering energy flowed into the sea beneath us, a million phosphorescent turquoise, emerald, and copper particles. We had to shield our eyes as each brilliantly colored wave crested and broke over the rail and across the deck. Something began to happen. We were moving forward—not tossed haphazardly—more like being powerfully sucked into a current. Marni stood transfixed, her noble features turned to stone like an ancient statue.

In fact, we were being towed, drawn by the

peculiar magnetic pull of the specter ship, first slowly, battered by the waves and chunks of ice, then continually gaining speed. And the water we took on board—the swells that should have filled our hull and taken us down—the liquid swirled into all the nooks and crannies of our ship, transforming every timber that it touched, reknitting and fusing each splintered fiber and grain until the *Lucy P. Simmons* was whole again! And the black ship, its hull split open like a coconut on a rock, began to slide back into the sea like a harpooned whale until its stern hit the ocean surface. We ran forward and stared at its shattered frame, now covered in a swarm of glittering particles, melding back together, plank to plank, beam to beam. The square-rigger creaked and groaned as it too reared back, whole again.

Suddenly, the sails of the specter ship began to whip and snap, faster and faster. The motion generated a whirlwind of warm air that whooshed around the *Lucy P.* like a cocoon, increasing in intensity until we found ourselves in the eye of a cyclone. The balmy air whirled over and around us, thawing our hands and feet. Ice melted off every surface, trickling this way and that.

No one moved to grab the wheel or hoist a sail—we knew we were no longer in control. The maelstrom of tepid air increased, blurring every-thing, until all that was visible was a sheath of rapidly spinning mist. The air current swept beneath us—the ship rocked side to side until the force of the tempest lifted the entire hull up and out of the water.

We fell to our knees, covering our eyes with the backs of our forearms, squinting into the mag-nificent display of fireworks—all except Grady, who stood, electrified, a wet spot expanding across the front of his pants. Rasjohnny, crouched beside Javan, began pummeling the deck with his palms, and chanting in a joyous mumbo mantra.

The whirring sound of the cyclone escalated into a single pitch as we shot forward, a pitch I rec-ognized—it was D.

There was a gentle sinking sensation, as the dazzling tunnel of air slowed to a whisper and dis-sipated.

The hull of the ship kissed the water once again, and as it did, the D note blossomed into a melody—D–D–F–A–G–F–G–E–C–D!

25

Soft edged and blurred like a dream, the world changed. The sea was blue and so was the sky, the temperature comfortably warm, wind steady. There was a healthy snap and a flap, the sound of sails catching a gust. Land to the east, gulls overhead.

We were roused, strewn about the deck as though we'd melted onto whatever spot we'd been standing when the ships collided. Rasjohnny and Javan stirred from a heap beside the lifeboats, Coleman crawled to his feet upon the poop deck. The Reds, slumped together at odd angles against the door to the companionway, slowly untangled their arms and legs. Tonio sat back-to-back with Irish, both of them rubbing their eyes with their fists. The cap'n took Addie by the hands and drew her to her feet, as though inviting her to dance. Pugsley shook himself off, sniffing and nosing Walter, Georgie, Annie, and me into consciousness. Our tattered, soaked clothing and equally ravaged faces were now dry and warm, no worse for wear. The castaways from the black ship were nowhere to be seen, having been either sucked back onto their own vessel or lost at sea. The enormity of what had transpired finally sunk in—how close we'd come to disaster, how my hopes of reuniting with Aunt Pru were nearly dashed.

Marni alone did not revive with the same tranquillity as the rest. With a violent start she sat up, a stricken look flashing across her face. Her hands flew to her throat, fingers fluttering, her breath coming in short gasps. The silver locket that hung at her throat—it was gone.

"Marni," I whispered. She was already on hands and knees, frantically pawing the deck, sweeping every surface. Panic rose in me. "We'll find it," I said, thinking how the waves had carried off much bigger things than a silver locket and chain. "We'll find it—I promise."

Walter, Georgie, and Annie joined in the search.

Against all odds I spotted it, the chain broken, tangled and snared on the end of a thick, bristling piece of rope. The hinged locket hung open like a small book. "Here!" I yelled, staring at the mysterious contents. Both sides were covered with a thin layer of glass; behind each was a complicated design woven from hair—blond hair, so fair as to be almost white. Intricately swirled and interlaced with great skill and care. Whose hair was it, and why did it mean so much to her? So strange to feel that I knew her so well, and yet so little.

I gently detached the chain with its dangling charm, and pressed both into Marni's open palm. Her eyes closed for a moment as she brought the precious token to her lips and bestowed on it a reverential kiss. "Thank you," she murmured, her composure and dignity returning. "Thank you," she repeated, to me, to God, or to both, I wasn't sure.

Slowly we all drifted together, side by side along the rail, incredulous, staring alternately at the horizon and at one another. Another crisis somehow averted. Walter draped one arm around me, the other around Georgie. Annie and Pugsley wiggled in between us. Marni and Addie too.

"T'ank the Lord!" Addie said, blessing herself. "We all survived!"

"Quaide," I said. "He escaped. I saw him climb aboard the black ship." Georgie's eyes widened and Walter pulled him close. "Of course," I whispered, so Georgie wouldn't hear, "he may be dead. Drowned."

"No," Marni said, staring out to sea. "He's out there with his mates. I feel it, sure as I feel these timbers strong beneath my feet. Things are exactly as they should be."

"That storm—or whatever it was—in all my years at sea, I've never seen the likes of it," the cap'n said quietly, shaking his head.

Grady stood, peering out over the ocean with his one good eye. "Me, I was fer certain that schooner was the *Dutchman* . . . that we was doomed. But it ain't true—can't be. What we was, was saved!" He shifted his gaze from Rasjohnny to me, and back, his face a question.

Marni, energized again by her talisman, leveled him a droll look. "Your instincts and respect for the supernatural were always correct—except now you see how the source of mystery can also bring about good if the recipients have their hearts in the right place! We have much to be thankful for!"

"The lady's right," one of the Reds exclaimed.

"We two are nothin' but grateful." Tonio made the sign of the cross. Irish removed his cap. Coleman raised his eyes skyward.

Cap'n looked at all of us, his eyes settling a moment longer on Addie than the rest. "Sea is full of mystery, that's for certain. So is life."

Irish interrupted. "Mystery? Here's the mystery! Where in tarnation are we? And what happened to the square-rigger?"

"Get the sextant," Cap'n commanded. Georgie ran off, scampered back, and produced the instrument. "No idea about the time of day," Cap'n said, "but it appears to be midmorning—my best guess." He pointed the device at the horizon, into the sun, pressed the clamp, and studied the sun's position. Coleman handed him a chart of some kind. After some quick calculations Cap'n whispered, "Thirty-five degrees, fifty minutes south of the equator . . ." He paused, made an adjustment, and continued his reckoning. "A hundred and thirty-seven degrees, twenty minutes east of the meridian?"

Coleman's eyes widened and his lips strained. "Aw . . ." he stammered. Swallowed. Opened and closed his mouth, like a big fish. "Aw . . ." The sound choked and died on his lips. We all stared, silently rooting for him to articulate whatever was stuck on his lips. Coleman closed his eyes, took a deep breath, opened his mouth, and sang in a deep surprising baritone, the syllables rolling smoothly over three lovely notes, *"Aus–tral–ia!"*

Marni's eyebrows lifted into a pair of silver arches. "Yes, Coleman! Kangaroo Island, of course! Not even a day's sail to Adelaide! Lucy, sweet, we're here! This is Australia!"

26

We followed the buoys set out in the channel, leading us into Port Adelaide. The entrance to the harbor was nearly concealed by groves of peculiar trees, their gnarly gray roots exposed above wavy sea grass and mudflats. There were as many curved and grasping roots along the water as there were branches reaching to the sky. "Deez trees called mangroves!" Javan called. "Got 'em on da islands too."

A tall flagpole stood like a lone sentry on a distant beach. Cap'n tipped his hat and announced, "Just north of Holdfast Bay!" That same flag must have waved at my aunt Pru upon her arrival! My heart thumped as the rooftops and spires of a city began to paint the horizon.

Annie, standing on a crate for a better look, clapped her hands. "Finally!" she exclaimed, dancing from one foot to the other. "We're here!" Georgie dashed to the rail, whooping like a banshee, Pugsley racing at his heels.

Addie grabbed hold of my hands and spun me in a circle. "Is there anything atall me girl can't accomplish when she puts 'er mind to it?"

Cleating a sail, one of the Reds hollered, "Hey there, Miss Lucy, how's it feel to fine'ly arrive in the land down under?" I could only nod, the unexpected rush of emotion rendering me speechless.

To the north and west the city had sprung up along the Port River and Inner Harbour, the sprawl of the metropolis to the south. We dropped anchor a ways offshore. Already a transport taxi was putt-putting in our direction.

Suddenly, I felt weak. Leaving the *Lucy P. Simmons*? The horrible realization turned my knees to jelly, my mouth, cottony dry. I leaned back against the rail, its sturdy timbers supporting me. How at home I'd become aboard our magnificent vessel! Heading off into the outback had seemed a fuzzy, far-off eventuality. I realized I didn't want to leave the comfortable familiarity of the ship. For my entire life its walls and floors, then decks and masts had cradled me. Here, a trace of Mother, there, my father's handprint. The ship, too, seemed pained at the thought of my departure, its creaking and groaning suddenly more audible above the surf. Marni's piercing green eyes took all this in. My gaze met hers for an instant, and I looked away. The transport boat tooted its cheery horn—*woot! Woot!* "Taxi, mates?" its skipper hollered.

"Not just yet," Marni called back. "Another couple of hours and we'll be ready!"

"Hooroo then!" He saluted. "Back around later!" My face must have betrayed my relief.

"Having second thoughts," Marni asked quietly. "Only natural. Nothing wrong with that, unless it paralyzes you."

That was exactly how I felt. Paralyzed.

She looped her elbow through mine, leading me back toward the stern, as though we were taking our morning constitutional. "You know, Lucy, there's no one aboard this ship who wouldn't call you brave."

I slapped away the tear that slid down my cheek.

"Remember, brave doesn't mean fearless. Courage means moving forward in the face of fear. Embracing hope. That's what we're going to do!

Collect our things, secure the ship, come ashore, make a plan. Just as we did back in Boston."

I took a ragged breath. "But are you sure—"

"Yes," she interrupted. "We'll find Pru—of course we will! Thanks to you we have the deed to the property—we know where she lives! You think we came this far for nothing?" Her fingers went to her necklace, expertly repaired by Coleman. She ran the locket back and forth along the chain.

"That locket . . ."

"Precious to me," she said. "Gives me what I need to go on . . ."

"Like my flute. My spyglass."

"Exactly."

I felt a great rush of love for this woman who had mysteriously found her way into my life. This woman who in some ways I knew so well, and in other ways knew not at all. I hesitated, then thought about what she'd said—going on even when you're afraid. I inhaled deeply. "It was open when I found it. The hair . . . ?"

Her eyes changed color, like the sea. Took on that distant, clouded look. "My son. I had—*have*—a son. His first haircut . . ."

"What happened to him? Where . . ." I thought of that first day with the cap'n, the two of them talking about going to sea to discover or replace things lost. The ship's bell began to clang.

"If we spend all day talking we'll never get to shore." She dropped my arm, squeezed my hand, and was off. Frustrated, I stared off toward land, the details still blurred by embarrassed tears. Walter came up alongside me. "You okay?"

"And why *wouldn't* I be okay!" I snapped, mortified to have him witness my trepidation.

"Sor-*ry*!" he said, emphasizing the last syllable, turning on his heel.

"Walter!" I called after him. He just kept walking.

I sighed. This was no way to begin.

"Lucy, Walter, Addie—Georgie, Annie!" Marni called the family roll. "Let's meet—my stateroom!"

Happy to have something decided for me, I headed to the companionway and down the stairs. Our little group assembled, Walter avoiding my eyes. I sat beside him, poked him with my elbow. Mouthed the word *Sorry*. Raised a hopeful eyebrow. He shrugged, focusing his attention on an invisible hangnail. The rest took seats, their excitement unnerving me.

"Well," Marni began. "Congratulations all around! We've accomplished the first part of our mission!" Addie stood and applauded, Annie and Georgie joined in. Walter and I added an obligatory clap or two. "So, now we need a plan, don't we? Prudence is near Alice Springs—I've done a bit of reading—the closest town is called Stuart. When we go ashore, we'll inquire as to the best way to get there. This much I know—it's a very long distance across the desert, through Aboriginal lands—a great frontier. Obviously, we can't all make the trek."

Annie's face fell. "I wanna go . . ."

"Yes," Marni said, "but who'll watch our ship? Care for Ida and the chickens?"

"Oh, Ida," Annie said, her small brow creased. She *tsk-tsk*ed, considering, shaking her head like one of her persnickety hens.

"Well, I'm goin'!" Georgie cried, arms crossed. His words, however, belied his expression. He looked hesitantly between his sister and Walter.

Marni paused. "I'd suggest that Lucy, Walter, and I make the journey. Addie, the cap'n, Annie, and, most of all, Georgie stay behind to guard the *Lucy P.*" The ship's bell clanged, as if affirming the idea.

An army of thoughts tramped across Georgie's face. "I can keep the ship safe!" he announced. "After all, I fought off a pirate, right, Lucy?" I gave him a thumbs-up. "And I'll take care of Annie—Walter, you'll see!"

Annie stuck out her bottom lip. "I'm not a

baby!" she retorted. At the same time she sidled up to Georgie.

"No, you're not a baby," Walter said. "You're brave and smart. Together with Georgie you'll make a great team until we return!"

"You promise to come back?" Annie asked, her eyes wide. "Promise?" Georgie, too, was suddenly attentive.

"From the bottom of my heart!" Walter said, holding his right hand up in an oath. Then he gathered the two of them and hugged them close.

"Addie?" Marni asked.

"Sounds a good plan to me, it does. And I'm certain the cap'n'd think it grand to spend some time ashore with the children." And with you, Addie, I thought. I pondered how the cap'n had lost his family—how Walter and the children had lost theirs, and how I'd lost mine. Pru, hers. And Marni . . . how new families were somehow brought together. For the first time since Mother's and Father's deaths, I felt a part of something real and lasting. A warm feeling spread through my chest.

"In addition," Marni went on, "our traveling party should include another male. Best to hire one of the crew. We know their characters and abilities. Lucy, whom do you suggest?"

The Reds were out since they only traveled

together. Rasjohnny and Javan—another pair not to be separated. Grady traveling through Aboriginal tribal lands could prove disastrous, even after his change of heart. Tonio or Irish—I just couldn't imagine them anywhere but at sea.

"Coleman," I said finally. "Let's ask Coleman."

"Exactly what I was thinking," Marni said, clearly pleased. "Walter? Are you with us?"

He looked at his brother and sister. "Georgie—that would make you the man of the family for a while. I know you can do it." Georgie puffed up with pride. Annie took his hand and snuggled next to Addie, Ida butting between them.

"Then I'm in!" Walter said. I fought the urge to throw my arms around him.

"Excellent!" Marni said. "I'll talk to the cap'n. Then we'll head to shore, find out what we need, secure passage one way or the other, and get on with it. In the meantime, Lucy, Walter—collect up only what you absolutely need. Best to travel light."

Back in my cabin I laid open a large leather bag. Retrieved the necessary things. The stocks I'd leave with Addie. I picked up the cards, glanced at the ivory box sitting on the shelf holding the rest of the deck. Should Annie keep them? As if reading my mind, the volatile kings and queens flipped from my hand and, like acrobats, somersaulted into the leather satchel. The lid of the case began to clatter and shimmy toward the edge of the shelf. I swiped it before it fell and tucked it in my traveling bag. Annie would be upset, but she'd get over it. Father's spyglass and flute, of course. Dungarees, two cotton shirts. Socks. Undergarments. Most important of all—Aunt Pru's letter and the deed to Grandfather's land.

It seemed like no time before the whistle of the taxi boat sounded, and Marni, Walter, Coleman, and I climbed down the rope ladder to be spirited ashore.

"Welcome to 'Stralia!" the skipper called. "The name is Reggie." He held out a sunburned hand and vigorously shook each of ours. "First time down under?"

"We're headed to Stuart," Marni began.

Reggie whistled. "Stuart?! What the devil's in Stuart that would possess ya t' take such a journey? Gotta cross the desert . . . the dang flies. Snakes. Not to mention the heat . . . ain't a soul out there but the natives. Red sand, dingoes, and, of course, the 'roos."

"'Roos?" Walter asked.

"Kangaroos, mate!" Reggie must have finally noticed our shock. "Well, it'll be an adventure," he quipped, skillfully maneuvering the boat toward the wharf. "Have ya arranged passage?"

Coleman shook his head.

"You'll need to train north to Port Augusta, head into one of the Ghan towns."

"Ghan towns?" Walter repeated.

"Where the Afghans live and keep their camels."

"Camels?" Walter sounded like a parrot.

"How else d'ya think you'll get yourselves 'cross the desert?" Reggie asked. We looked at one another, incredulous. "Only safe way to Stuart. Train won't take ye, and the trip would kill a horse. But the cameleers'll get ye there. Well, here we be, mates! Maclaren Wharf! Good luck to y'all! From sailin' ship to the ships of the desert!" He tipped his wide-brimmed hat and grinned.

I barely noticed the bustling activity along the wharf or St. Vincent Street. Camels—ships of the desert? Snakes? Flies? Dingoes? My head was abuzz. It didn't take more than a couple of additional inquiries to confirm that Reggie was right. The only way to Stuart was by caravan.

We purchased the same broad-brimmed hats as Reggie wore, the only difference being the corks bobbing around the brim to shoo the flies. Netting, and swags—rolled canvas cases housing a thin mattress, with a fold-back flap to keep out the mice and the snakes—a necessity for sleeping under the stars. Canteens. Balm to protect our fair skin from the desert sun. A map.

We didn't waste any time. Probably Marni understood that hesitation might grow into doubt, and doubt into fear. Our supplies skillfully wrapped and stacked on the pier, Marni hailed Reggie's water taxi and accompanied him back to collect the rest of our supplies on ship, and to bring Addie, the cap'n, Georgie, Annie, and Pugsley to shore to bid us farewell.

27

We smelled them before we saw them—at least a hundred ornery camels, some shuffling about, others hunkered down on spindly legs bent at odd angles. It was just as Reggie said. The Ghan town—a hodgepodge of rough tin shacks, a peculiar wooden structure they called the mosque at one end. A caravan of thirty beasts laden with huge sacks of grain, water barrels, parcels of every size and shape tied to their lumpy bodies, was lumbering out, the camels strung together like desert beads on a thick rope. I saw a rocking chair strapped to one of them, a collection of copper pots and pans on another. Dusky-skinned turbaned men in dungarees moved between them, expertly coaxing the beasts with a poke, a pull, or a jab. In response, the creatures would curl back their lips, revealing rows of long knobby teeth and lolling pink tongues.

"Lady! Lady!" a jaunty cameleer yelled, waving both hands at Marni. The bearded fellow had dark lively eyes, his head wrapped round and round in a lightweight cotton turban, fringe hanging from one side. He wore a blousy white shirt topped with a colorful woven vest. Dust-covered dungarees and sand-scuffed leather boots completed his attire. "Best camels! Come see!" He led an impressive beast toward us. The dromedary wore a tasseled headpiece with a shiny brass medallion embellishing the spot between its ears. A Persian carpet was thrown over its hump, an ornate leather saddle perched atop it. A beaded harness laden with tarnished brass bells circled its head. "How many you? Four? You come with Farzad for best ride!" He flashed a brilliant white smile. "Where you go to?"

Marni extended a hand, which Farzad took and vigorously pumped. "Stuart," she said. "A homestead near Alice Springs. Can you take us there?"

"Oh, yes, Lady, Farzad take you."

In no time at all, arrangements were made,

the camels brought about, and our bags strapped on. After a brief lesson on how to ride, Farzad uttered some unintelligible command, and, accompanied by a chorus of peculiar grunting sounds—*nuuuuuuuuuuuur!*—Huma, my camel, lifted her back haunches. Then, the unfolding of the front legs, and up . . . up . . .

In an instant we were towering over the ground. The strange loping rhythm of the camels was not unlike the rolling of a ship in gentle seas. A breeze buffeted my face. We headed out, two by two, Walter and me side by side, Marni and Coleman behind. "Aunt Pru, here I come!" I whispered.

Walter reached across and squeezed my hand. "Last leg of the journey!" he exclaimed, his eyes full of delight.

Sadly, our excitement was short-lived. It was hotter than hot. The flies relentless. Day after endless day we rode across paprika-colored sand, through tufts of spinifex grass, each of its thin blades razor sharp.

Hours ran into days, and days into weeks. Sweat poured in steady streams. The only one of us who didn't seem to mind was Coleman, who passed the time entertaining us with every song he knew—and he knew hundreds. It was amazing that someone who couldn't speak could sing so fluently. Every chantey he'd ever heard he'd memorized, taking delight in being able to sing what he couldn't say:

> *"Can't you hear the gulls a-callin'? Only one more*
> *day a-furlin'*
> *Only one more day a-cursin'—Oh, heave and sight*
> *the anchor, Johnny,*
> *For we're close aboard the port, Johnny."*

One night, as Farzad prepared for our supper, Coleman sang, *"I'm so hungry I could eat a horse!"* At first I thought this melodic snippet was part of just one more peculiar song, but when my eyes met his I saw he was waiting for a response.

Marni smiled and sang back in a voice surprisingly lush and low, *"Me, too! How about you, Lucy?"*

I took a deep breath and improvised a two-note tune: *"You bet!"*

"Crazy Yanks," Farzad exclaimed. Then he corrected himself, singing in a nasal tone, *"You crazy Yanks!"* We all applauded, the sound echoing across the vast open space.

For three weeks more we trekked through red sand and massive rusty rock formations, past ghost gum trees with peeling white bark, around gnarly, gray, dead trees littering the ground like desert driftwood. And still, it seemed to me we were no closer to our destination. We hadn't passed another caravan in more than a week. Farzad stopped several camel lengths in front of us, and appeared to be deliberating on which way to go.

"Do you think we're lost?" I whispered. Marni stared into the distance, biting her lower lip. Walter frowned.

"Farzad—when will we get to Stuart?" Coleman sang.

Farzad reined in his camel and spun around, shaking his head so angrily his cheeks jiggled. "Why you ask that? You don't trust Farzad? No you sing now!" he barked, pointing a trembling finger.

We exchanged doubtful glances and followed, but our confidence in him waned and disappeared like the water in our canteens. Consulting the map we'd brought proved useless, as there were no real landmarks to establish our location. Food was scarce—we were hungry, thirsty, and exhausted. Could it be we'd come this far across the sea only to be lost in the desert? That the grasp of the curse had stretched across the water and over the sand?

The worst moment of all was when we wound up back at a spot we'd been before—facing a striated canyon of brick-colored stone, palms and ghost gums at its base.

"You've led us in a circle!" Walter shouted. I'm

sure he would've throttled Farzad, if he'd had the strength.

"You no like, get off camel and go," Farzad retorted.

"Look!" I exclaimed, shielding my eyes with one sunburned hand. At first I thought the faint wavering outline of a small camel train threading its way along the precipice of the canyon might just be a mirage. But staring at it, I experienced a pull, deep in my chest.

Huma must have felt it too. Without so much as a tug on the reins, she turned and started toward it, with all but Farzad following. I barely noticed his ranting as we left him there, so focused was I on the three ghostly riders draped head to toe in flowing wispy robes. Their silhouettes flickered against the backdrop of red rock and sky, nearly transparent, more of a suggestion than a reality. The hypnotic effect of their spectral garb blowing in the breeze brought to mind the rippling sails of a phantom ship. Closer and closer we were drawn, as though reeled in by an invisible line.

At a distance of several camel lengths Huma stopped and we faced these unearthly travelers. They stared out from beneath the filmy shrouds that covered their faces, their features visible, but blurred, dream-like. *"Mother . . ."* I mouthed the word through dry lips, unable to produce a sound.

"Yes, darling . . ." I felt the words rather than heard them, soft, like a gentle breeze against my face. Beside her, Father gazed at me, his veiled features a mingling of pride and sadness. I wanted to dismount, to run to them, but I knew this was a divide I could not cross. It took me several long moments to drag my attention from them to take in the third phantom rider. He grinned slyly. Of course! The king of diamonds.

The threesome reined their animals around and took the lead, seemingly gliding above the surface of the arid red earth. I cast a look back over my shoulder to assure that Marni, Walter, and Coleman were still behind me. Wide-eyed and silent they rode along while Farzad hightailed it in the opposite direction, kicking up a cloud of dust in his wake. Our untouchable guides led the way, always well in front, an unbridgeable gap between us.

To our right, off in the distance, I spotted two more white-clad specter cameleers, one riding tall and regal, the other short and lumpy. I knew, even from their faint, shadowy profiles, who they were— the queen of spades and the queen of diamonds.

This entourage escorted us across miles and miles of wasteland, in a rhythm all their own. Strangely, there was no need to stop for reprieve or sustenance of any kind. Day and night blended together in a constant glowing twilight, as though time was standing still. We trekked on, inexplicably refreshed, our stamina never diminishing. That, and the great relief I felt—the fact that they revealed themselves to all of us had to mean that their existence was no longer a secret I was bound to keep.

Then, as the sun finally began to rise, their images began to quiver and become less and less clear, until they dissipated like morning mist. We gasped as we found ourselves alone, overcome with a powerful hunger and thirst, in an even stranger landscape than the one we'd been in.

Our sure-footed camels picked their way across a flat open space, tufts of spinifex grass here and there, the paprika-colored earth pitted with craters. Holes, three feet wide by at least six feet deep, had been dug just about everywhere, the loose soil piled haphazardly around the perimeter.

"Where are we?" Walter asked.

"*Holy, holy, holy, Lord God Almighty,*" Coleman sang. Marni chuckled.

"This is a *whole* different kind of holy!" I said, and we all laughed. Nervous laughter. Why had they led us here, only to leave us?

"Stop right there! Where do ye think yer goin'?"

A man had appeared out of nowhere, leveling a rifle at us. He squinted through the scope, walking closer and closer.

"You can put that down," Marni said. "We mean you no harm. The fact is, we're lost. On our way to Stuart."

The man lowered the gun a smidgen. "And what would bring you to Stuart?"

"I'm looking for my aunt Prudence."

He cocked his head. Stepped back, lowered his firearm. He studied me, a parade of expressions tramping across the ruddy, sun-weathered face beneath his wide-brimmed hat.

"Prudence," he said.

"Prudence Simmons."

"Ye look to be her spittin' image," he exclaimed. "Didn't realize she was expectin' visitors. Aiden Murray," he continued, extending his hand. "Care-taker." I'd forgotten about the flute in my pocket until it began to hum. "Yep, this is the homestead, all right. The holes?" He shook his head. "Crazy talk about buried treasure. Hell on the livestock, and not a trinket or silver coin to be found!"

"We're actually here? My aunt is here?" Relief washed over me.

"Come on," Aiden said. "I'll take ye to the ranch. Look like ye can use a little grub, a hot shower." We loped along behind him, his words like a balm to me. "First belonged to the grandfather. Before my time. A real character—gold prospector, then made a fortune in the opal mines. When he went back to the island, my family was left in charge. Raised sheep. Cattle."

"The island?" I asked.

"Emerald Isle," Aiden replied. "Ireland. Died on the crossin' is how I heard it. Ship went down—took 'is secrets with 'im. My family's been 'ere ever since. Miss Prudence saw fit to keep us on, happy to say. One hell of a woman, that one! Our arrangement's worked well, except for these blasted holes."

Baaaaaaaa! For an instant I expected to see Ida. Instead, a long-haired, dirty-white sheep bleated from inside a crater. "See what I mean?" Aiden said, throwing himself on his belly and hoisting the dumb beast up by her front legs. The sheep scrambled off and we continued on.

Finally, behind a small grove of ghost gums, a long low ranch house appeared. It had a peaked metal roof and white gingerbread trim around the deep covered porch that ran the length of the building. A set of double doors was set dead center, floor-to-ceiling windows on either side.

We dismounted on wobbly knees, and Aiden led the camels to a corral beside the barn. Marni squeezed my shoulder. Walter stretched and casually ran his hand under the hair at the nape of my neck, giving it a tousle. Coleman hung back, whistling a senseless meandering tune through his teeth. Aiden returned, and hopped up the steps to the house.

My heart thumped uncontrollably. After all this time, I'd never actually imagined how this would be. Aiden raised a huge iron knocker and rapped it several times. "Aiden, here," he called. "Got ye some visitors, Miss Prudence!"

"Visitors! Who in the world . . ." The voice wafted through the windows, rendering me weak. Tears welled. Marni and Walter pushed me forward as the door swung open.

28

She started out, then froze, her smile dropping into open-mouthed awe—or perhaps shock. One hand flew to her lips and she grabbed hold of the railing with the other. "Lucy?! Lucy, is it really you?" She flung her arms wide and I took the steps two at a time. In an instant I was in her embrace, so tight it left me breathless. I smelled her lemony curls, falling across my shoulders and mingling with my own. Her hands flew over my face and hair, then down along my arms, as if to confirm that I was real. Finally, she held me at arm's length, devouring me in an incredulous once-over.

"The letter they sent said you were *dead*!" she cried. "Drowned—all of you!" A furtive look swept across her face as her gaze shifted over my shoulder. "Edward! Edward and Johanna?"

I touched her hand. One look at me and she knew. "The curse! Of course!" She wrapped her arms around me again and buried her face in my neck. "Well, thank God for you! A miracle!" She sat back and ran her fingers through her hair. Grabbed hold of my hands and squeezed, as if concerned that if she let go I might disappear. "I'm seeing you, touching you, and still it's hard for me to take in!" She glanced at Marni, Walter, and Coleman.

"My family—yours now too," I said. "Marni, who rescued me—twice—from the sea—and Walter. Walter's sister and brother, and Addie—we left them back in Adelaide with our ship. And this is Coleman. He sings!"

"Pleased to make your acquaintance," he crooned, bowing deeply.

"I'll be off then," Aiden said, "to bring in your bags. Then there's sheep to shear and the like . . ."

With a friendly wave Pru sent him on his way. I saw her suddenly, as my friends must have. Tall. Willowy. Nothing demure or reserved about her. Her hair, a long wild mane of unruly red curls that refused to be tamed into a bun or braid. It gave her a wild, feline look—like a lion. She was smartly dressed in tailored beige linen trousers and a flowing white blouse, a large opal pendant at her throat. The legs of her trousers were rolled to mid-calf, revealing tightly laced, high brown boots. A brimmed leather hat hung behind her at the ready. Stacks of gold and silver bangle bracelets jingled at her wrists each time she gestured dramatically, which she did every time she spoke—an arresting accompaniment to her words. "In!" she commanded. "So much to tell, I can hardly wait. . . ." She led us into a spacious room, sparsely decorated. A simple sofa and a number of oak rocking chairs, a Persian rug, a kangaroo pelt hanging on the wall beside built-in bookshelves. Coleman's eyes lit up at the upright piano in one corner.

First she tended to our aching bodies. The luxury of a warm bath—clean hair, skin free of dust and sweat! The scent of lavender instead of the musky, dank smell of camel! Each of us was assigned a room, with a snug bed wrapped in crisp white sheets. Clean clothes were produced, some-thing to fit each of us. Tea in the kettle. Scones on china plates. A bowl of fruit. Soup on the stove. Flowers in a vase.

Around the table we did our best not to gulp and guzzle, but, oh, the taste of civilized food! Pru laughed, taking obvious pleasure in satisfying our great hunger and thirst. A walk about the property and outbuildings. When the combination of ample food and deep fatigue set in, Marni, Coleman, and Walter retired for their first comfortable night of sleep since we'd left the *Lucy P.* Pru and I lingered, wanting to stretch a few more minutes out of this amazing day. Finally, when my yawns became as prevalent as words, Pru led me to my room. Tucked in, lying in the enveloping darkness, I gazed at my aunt in the doorway, silhouetted in the light from the hall, her hair framing her face in a halo of bronze. "Good night, Lucille," she said quietly.

"'Night, Aunt Pru."

She remained a moment or two more, the two of us memorizing each other again before she quietly closed the door.

The next day, all of us quite revived, Pru, Walter, Coleman, and Marni got to know one another better, describing the way the paths of our lives crossed. We shared the full scope of our adventure around the breakfast table—a morning meal that lasted until lunch! Coleman sat, riveted, hearing, for the first time, along with Pru, the story of the day it all began—Father, Mother, and I going for a sail, the storm rolling in, the Brute—Walter's father—in his capsized boat, the attempted rescue. I relived it all again, the near drowning, the incessant barking of our beloved Pugsley, being overtaken by the icy water, waking to find Aunt Margaret and Uncle Victor in charge . . . my mouth filled with bitterness at the memory. I watched Pru's face as I spoke of the magic of my parent's love that protected me, and saw nothing but wonder. Her eyes flashed when she heard how her wretched brother sent me away to Marni, then gratitude transformed her features upon hearing of Marni's care, and shock at the account of the final storm that sent our mansion crashing into the sea. Coleman, too, blinked his eyes in astonishment at the saga he found himself part of. He gestured toward me, singing, *"Bravest gal I ever did see—a heart as big as the ocean . . ."* Marni and Walter added details about the transformation of mansion to ship, and the trials, tribulations, and supernatural aspects of our voyage.

Pru reached across the table and covered my hand with her own. "I'm so sorry I wasn't there for you—that you had to endure all of this alone!" An array of emotions flashed across her face—sadness. Anger. Stubborn determination.

Walter glanced from Pru to me, and back. "Sometimes you two look so much alike I think I'm seeing double!"

I smiled, and placed my other hand on top of

Pru's. "We're in this together now," I said. "That's all that matters!"

"At last," Pru answered, "someone in my family who shares my quest! Lucille—you and I *will* discover the secret to unlock this curse, the consequences of which can no longer be denied!"

"Yes." I nodded emphatically.

Marni rose. "I'm sure you two Simmons women have much to discuss in private. The rest of us can entertain ourselves for a bit."

Pru nodded toward the piano. "Perhaps Coleman can provide some musical recreation while Lucy and I retire to the study?" In an instant he was seated at the upright, arms outstretched, his graceful fingers poised above the keys. He began to play, his hands so better suited to music than they were to seafaring. As Pru and I left the room he launched into one song after another. *"She's only a bird in a gilded cage, A beautiful sight to see, You may think she's happy and free from care, She's not, though she seems to be . . ."*

Pru blushed slightly and grinned, looking every bit a lovely rare bird, minus the cage, of course. She ushered me into the study, toward a long library table covered in neat piles of books and papers. "Come around," she said, spreading them out. We sat, side by side. She gathered a yellowed stack and thumbed through them. "Here—birth, marriage, and death certificates . . ." She indicated a pile on the right. "Land records, wills, legal forms." She unrolled a fragile parchment. "Our family tree." She spoke quietly, intensely, her eyes riveted to the page, smoothing it with strong yet graceful fingers.

I stared at the document, fascinated. There was my name, under Mother's and Father's, the words *Died at sea* penciled in beneath each. As if on cue, Coleman's voice rang out: *"Strike the bell, second mate! Let us go below. Look away to windward! You can see it's going to blow . . ."*

Pru took a pen, and in time with the jaunty chantey, made a triumphant slash through the dire proclamation following my name.

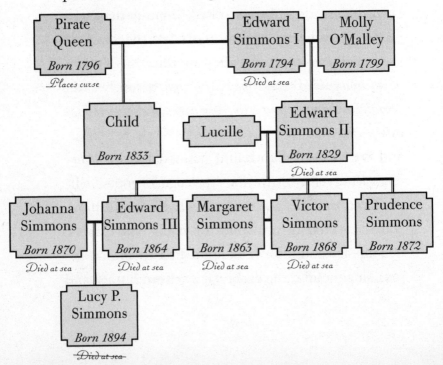

Pirate Queen — Born 1796 — *Places curse*

Edward Simmons I — Born 1794 — *Died at sea*

Molly O'Malley — Born 1799

Child — Born 1833

Lucille

Edward Simmons II — Born 1829 — *Died at sea*

Johanna Simmons — Born 1870 — *Died at sea*

Edward Simmons III — Born 1864 — *Died at sea*

Margaret Simmons — Born 1863 — *Died at sea*

Victor Simmons — Born 1868 — *Died at sea*

Prudence Simmons — Born 1872

Lucy P. Simmons — Born 1894 — *Died at sea*

"Here's the story as I know it," Pru continued. "It all started with my grandfather—your great-grandfather—Edward Simmons the First."

"Yes," I said. "I'd found a letter you'd written to Father, locked in the safe."

"I retraced my grandfather's steps. From his hometown in Ireland to here. Old-timers remembered tales of the huge treasure he stole, rumors about a family curse, but not a one was privy to the details of his pirate queen, or the baby they produced. Then, there's this." She retrieved a ragged scrap of paper, with a rough grid penciled in, letters across the top, numbers down the side. An x was scrawled in box J3. "I found it here, stashed in a strongbox. I felt certain this marked the spot here on the homestead where Grandfather had buried the alleged stolen treasure and the rest of his holdings—and, more important, the answers we're seeking. But without a compass rose, there was no way to know how the grid was intended to lay out over the property." She shook her head and waved her open hands toward the heavens imploringly. "God knows, I tried it every which way, to no avail!" With this she threw herself forward in an exaggerated expression of frustration, her forearms and head thumping the desk. I patted her shoulder, recalling the cratered landscape and knowing how she felt, remembering my own vexation in trying to get into the safe. Pru sat up, squeezed my hand, and smiled, her whole face lighting up. "Difficult, yes, but together, I know, we'll figure this out!"

In the next room, Coleman sang on: *"Way-hay, up she rises! Way-hay, up she rises! Way-hay, up she rises, early in the morning . . ."*

Pru continued, suddenly serious, her brow furrowed in thought. "It's conceivable that this illegitimate child of their liaison is still alive—he or she would be some seventy-odd years old, and might be able to fill in the missing pieces."

"So, how can we find out?"

"That's what I've been trying to do. And I'm not the only one."

I raised an eyebrow. "What do you mean?"

"I've been followed, off and on, for the last few years. A scrappy-looking pirate and—"

I jumped in. "A green-eyed man?"

"Yes!" she exclaimed, springing from the chair. I told her about my near kidnapping, how the black square-rigger had followed us, about our collision rounding the Cape of Good Hope. Quaide's involvement and final disappearance. Her eyes narrowed and her nostrils flared.

"Somehow those scoundrels knew you'd

eventually lead them to me!"

"But why?" I asked. "What are they after?"

She ran both hands through her tumble of out-of-control locks. "The money, that's what. Edward the First was rolling in it—the stolen pirate treasure, booty from his days as a privateer. Opals and gold from his stint here as a prospector. There's a fortune to be had and I'm sure they saw us as the missing link that will steer them to it."

I thought of Quaide. Of course. It all fit. "We may have seen the last of them," I said, calling to mind how he'd crashed his way into the gaping hole of the capsized pirate ship, waves teeming in around him. And Marni's sense that Quaide wound up exactly where he needed to be— wherever that was.

"They're as clever and resourceful as they are devious," Pru said. "If there was any hope of survival, I'll bet they grabbed it. You could be right. They may have been no match for the sea—but I wouldn't count on it." She tipped her head to the side and nibbled the inside of her cheek. "More and more I feel that finding some record of the child they produced—Edward and the pirate queen—will somehow be the key to unlock this mystery." Suddenly my flute began to vibrate and hum. It levitated out of my pocket, sounding that mystery tune again, "D–D–F, A–G–F, G–E–C, D." A puff of glitter wafted in the air as it danced before us. Pru's mouth dropped open. "What in heaven's name?"

"Father's flute. It does this—it helped me figure out the combination to the safe."

Pru leaned forward, tipping her head, delight playing across her face. "You are remarkable!" she said, speaking directly to the lovely little instrument, tweaking it with her index finger. The flute became even more animated, showing off all the more, whistling and gyrating, improvising on the familiar melody, louder and louder with each repeated refrain.

In the next room, Coleman took up the tune, creating a spirited duet. Responding to this, the flute bobbed across the room toward the parlor. Pru grabbed my hand and danced the two of us out of the study to find Marni and Walter clapping along in time. As we sashayed in, the magical woodwind in the lead, their clapping abruptly stopped. Having never witnessed the antics of my flute before, they gaped at us, a mix of shock and amusement on their faces.

Suddenly, Coleman's voice rang out, clothing the familiar melody with words:

"This is the ballad of Mary Maude Lee—
a Queen and a Pirate—the Witch o' the Sea.
Tho' fair of face, and tho' slight of build,
many a seafarer's blood did she spill!
A la dee dah dah . . . a la dee dah dee,
This is the ballad of Mary Maude Lee."

I inhaled sharply. Pru looked up, a note of recognition flickering across her face. "I've heard this melody before," she whispered. "As a child . . ."

"She fired her blunderbuss, torched their tall
sails,
Laughing as mariners screamed, moaned, and
wailed.
Off with their silver! Off with their gold!
Off with supplies lying deep in their holds!
A la dee dah dah . . . a la dee dah dee,
This is the ballad of Mary Maude Lee."

The color drained from Marni's face. She gripped the arms of the chair with white knuckles. Coleman continued, the flute dancing in the air beside him, sounding a shrill descant. Pru, Marni, and I stood, riveted by the lyrics, Walter glancing from one of us to the other, his face a question.

"Her coffers grew fat, till Edward, that gent,
Escaped with her booty, and then off he went.
She swore her revenge against that sorry traitor,
Placed a curse on the sons of the cuss who
*   betrayed her!*
A la dee dah dah . . . a la dee dah dee,
The sons of his sons would all die in the sea!
A la dee dah dah . . . a la dee dah dee,
This is the ballad of Mary Maude Lee."

Coleman launched into a piano interlude between verses and suddenly there was a sound like a drumroll, building to the next chorus. Walter saw it first—the box of cards rising from my travel bag, the lid vibrating percussively. "What?" Walter asked. "What's going on?" I placed my hand on his arm, and raised an index finger to my lips. Taking a deep breath, Coleman continued,

"Mary Maude Lee said, 'I'll spit on their
*   graves!'*
Then drew back and spat in the white churning
*   waves.*
And each generation of menfolk that followed,
Into the sea they'd be chewed up and swallowed!

A la dee dah dah . . . a la dee dah dee,
This is the ballad of Mary Maude Lee."

I rushed to Marni, whose face collapsed, the life draining from it with each subsequent verse. Pru's and Walter's eyes were fixed on the box of cards, levitating and chattering, floating across the room. Coleman, oblivious, sang on,

"The only real way that the curse can be broken,
was revealed in the last words that Mary had
*   spoken,*
'If not in my lifetime, then to my descendants,
Hand over my treasure and appease Mary's
*   vengeance!'*
A la dee dah dah . . . a la dee dah dee,
This is the ballad of Mary Maude Lee!"

He ended with a great flourish, an arpeggio from the bottom of the keyboard to the top. Father's flute trilled on the final D note. The box of cards dropped to the ground with a bang. The deck shot out, splayed in a wild array across the polished floor. The face cards fluttered and rose, hovering around Marni.

Eyes wide, hands trembling, she plucked the queen of spades from the air and held it out before her. She stared at the image, gasped, and dropped it, as though it had burned her fingertips.

She sunk back into her chair, looked from one of us to the other. "Now it all makes sense," she said, her hand flying to her locket. "Mary Maude Lee . . . Mary Maude Lee was . . . my mother."

29

It took more than a moment for the enormity of her words to sink in. Marni—the daughter of my great-grandfather and the pirate queen! That meant that . . .

"You're related!" Walter exclaimed, eyes darting between us. "Marni is your . . . your . . ."

"My aunt," Pru said. "Lucy's great-aunt."

I ran, knelt, and flung my arms around Marni. Laid my head on her shoulder.

"My own mother," Marni whispered into my hair, "responsible for all this evil . . . it explains, of course, why I was drawn to you, unconsciously trying to undo her doings—it's what I've done my whole life, in one way or another. . . ."

The queen of spades flipped up. "Oh, please," she retorted, leaning off the card. "I offered you everything and you rejected it! Had you not been such an ingrate, your own boy might not have gotten snatched by that so-called husband of yours."

The room fell silent as they ogled the talking icon. Walter looked between the card and me, eyebrows raised. Coleman's mouth was agape, and Pru stood, riveted. Now they all shared in the secret I'd been bound to all these months. Marni's eyes narrowed. She picked the card up between thumb and index finger, flicked the image of her mother to the floor, and stamped it down with her foot.

Gently, Pru touched Marni's arm. "Did you know your father?"

Marni shook her head. "No. It was forbidden to speak of him. Didn't even know his name. I only knew he double-crossed her." She turned to Coleman. "And I never heard this ballad. Where did you learn it?"

He shrugged. *"Aboard some ship, across the Irish Sea . . . forgot about it until that crazy flute . . . crazy flute . . ."*

The bulldog-faced queen of diamonds shot into the air. "Now that you've got that witch under control, let's get on with it. The cards! How about the cards?"

"Now they're all talking!" Walter exclaimed, pointing at the animated card. Pru stared at the queen of diamonds. "I know you," she said. "You're my grandmother! Molly O'Malley!"

"Yes, yes," the queen responded, "love and kisses and all that hogwash. The cards! Are ya payin' attention to the cards?"

"So, it's all about the cards?" Pru asked, gesturing toward a far wall where a large framed display hung. About a dozen small rectangles had been cut into a matte, revealing a set of familiar designs. She turned to me. "My father had this deck of cards . . . my grandmother—her," Pru said, pointing, "the queen of diamonds—Father said she was handy with pen and ink. When Grandfather was off to sea, which was more often than not, she'd pass the days illustrating. She crafted a whole set of cards, with tiny scenes on the back of each."

"Impressive work, if I must say so myself," the double-chinned queen interjected.

"Father seldom took them out. My brothers coveted them," Pru continued, "but I wanted them all for myself. When Father refused to give them to me, I'm ashamed to say, I slipped a few from the deck. Not the most colorful, or the most interesting, just whatever I could grab. Took them with me when I left home, eventually had them framed."

"Reunited at last!" the queen of diamonds quipped.

Pru strode across the room, removed the frame from the wall. She peeled the backing and carefully extracted each card.

"Let's have a better look," Walter said. We gathered the cards from the floor. They felt electric in our hands. As I picked up the king of diamonds he smiled slyly. "Getting warmer," he whispered, and winked.

"Why not arrange them by suit," Walter suggested, "so we can see what's missing." We spread the cards on the table—there were fifty-one, thanks to Ida, plus two jokers. Everyone joined in, sorting them into neat stacks. The cards began to shimmer around the edges. The flute, which had settled on the music stand of the piano, began to hum, and Coleman provided a quiet accompaniment. Marni moved her foot, lifted the queen of spades, and shoved her into the proper pile. They were all there, except the jack of clubs, which might be still churning around in Ida's gut.

I attempted to pile the clubs atop the diamonds. The air between the stacks seemed charged, an invisible force repelling them. Suddenly the collection of spades dove from Marni's hands and landed with a snap atop the diamond pile.

"Try the clubs now," Walter said, his eyes aglow. Again I moved to pick up the clubs. This time my fingers met with a sudden shock.

"Ow!" I yanked away my hand, shaking out my tingling fingers.

"Hearts?" Marni suggested. "Red, black, red, black . . . ?"

Pru placed the hearts and then the clubs, the collection complete. The two jokers catapulted to the top of the pile, and the entire deck glowed.

"Maybe we're supposed to play with them," Walter joked. "Beggar-My-Neighbor? Gin rummy?" The cards purred. He went to cut the deck and *ZAP!* "I'm not dealing," he retorted, blowing on his fingers. The edge of the deck glimmered—teasing, taunting. I inched my fingers forward.

"Careful," Marni warned. The deck pulsed, as though ruffled by an invisible hand. I stared at the intricate drawing on the back of the joker—a castle set on a shoreline, overlooking the sea.

"Wait," I exclaimed, struck by an idea. With fingers atop the pile I slipped my thumb beneath and rapidly thrummed the stack from the bottom up.

Marni gasped. Pru leaned forward. "Lucy, you've got it!" Walter said. "Do it again!"

Quickly, evenly, I flipped the cards, the small explosion of displaced air whipping up an energy in the room that blew like a tempest, puffs of glittering mist exploding in colorful bursts. On the backs of the moving cards a picture story unfolded. Two ships, tiny characters having a duel, men carrying crates—no—chests! Making off with them. A woman waving a cutlass as the ship sails away. Onshore, men digging a hole on a hill beside the sea. A coffin? A chest? They laid it in the ground beside a church. The word *Clare* appeared in the clouds. We flipped the animated sequence over and over, until the story was clear. "Clare Island!" Pru cried. "Someone, or perhaps something, is buried on Clare Island!"

"Brilliant," Marni whispered. "Your grandmother created a kinetograph revealing the location of the treasure—or, if not the treasure, at least a valuable clue!"

Pru nodded, her cheeks flushed with excitement. She looked at me. "It was your mother's and father's love that flowed through the whole of this, guiding you along, inspiring magic of every kind. And now, thanks to them—and to you—all of you— we have the grid, and we know where to search! All the pieces are coming together!"

Marni stood, her strength and color revived.

Her fingers moved to the locket at her throat. "Your Edward and my mother began this. It's only right we join together in ending it. They just didn't see that whenever you seek vengeance, it always comes back to you. By cursing the Simmons clan my mother also cursed her own. My son—her grandson—wherever he is, is *both* a Simmons and a Lee! I just hope the sea hasn't already claimed him."

"We can do this!" I exclaimed, filled with new confidence. "Find the treasure! Locate Marni's son! Dispel the curse!"

I looked between Aunt Pru and Marni, then to Walter. Thought of Addie, Annie, and Georgie, and my beloved Pugsley, waiting back in Adelaide, our ship at the ready. An affectionate glance toward Coleman, who, in his inability to speak, had unknowingly revealed the source of the curse. I had everyone and everything I'd desired, and now a clear destination. *It's all in the cards, dear one.* Mother, as always, had been right.

"We've little time to waste!" I said.

"To Adelaide!" Walter declared.

Pru nodded vigorously. "Then on to Ireland—Clare Island!"

"I've never been more ready for anything," Marni asserted, her eyes sparkling with resolve.

Coleman sang, *"There's no stoppin' us now!"*

Aiden appeared at the door, perhaps drawn by the music, and found himself in a wave of excitement. "Is there anything you need me to do, miss?" he asked, clearly confused. He was addressing Pru, but I stepped forward. "We'll need a week or so to restore our strength and make a plan. We'll gather what we need. Then you can prepare the camels. Close the house."

"Indeed!" Pru exclaimed.

"Fill in those holes," Walter added.

"Crazy Yanks," Aiden muttered under his breath, heading back out the door.

Coleman turned to the piano and launched into a reprise of the tune that had led me this far. The flute joined in. We raised our voices on the refrain—even Walter. *"A la dee dah dah . . . a la dee dah dee . . ."*

And in a sudden burst of inspiration I improvised a final coda, singing out my fervent vow: *"'The last of my family's been lost to the sea!'"*

ACKNOWLEDGMENTS

An ocean of gratitude to the insightful, enthusiastic HarperCollins crew: Katherine Tegen, Claudia Gabel, Melissa Miller, and Alexandra Arnold. Thanks for believing in me enough to launch Lucy's story.

Also, thank you to Michael Dyer of the New Bedford Whaling Museum and to Bruce Williams, vice president of Captain's Cove, for sharing their expertise on tall ships and sailing—any inaccuracies in this regard are mine.

And lastly, great appreciation to Tom Lynch, for sharing his love of the sea and his willingness to dive into mystery.

A GLOSSARY OF
NAUTICAL TERMS

A

aft–area of the ship located behind the midpoint, near the stern

aloft–the upper rigging of a sailing ship, where work is often done

arsenic–a poisonous substance used to coat areas of the ship that are mostly underwater in order to prevent the growth of tiny organisms such as algae, barnacles, mollusks, and seaweed

B

batten down the hatches–to securely close all doors and hatchways during rough weather in order to keep out water

belaying pins–short metal or hardwood rods or pins used to secure (or belay) the rigging

bilge–an area in the bottom of the ship (in the hull) where accumulated water runs that must regularly be pumped out

boom–a spar (wooden pole) attached to the bottom of a sail

bow–the front part of the ship

bowsprit–a spar extending from the front of a ship

(bow) to hold rigging in place

broaching–when a sailing ship struggles to maintain its course and movement and must turn sharply

buntlines–the lines (ropes) fastened to the bottom of a sail used to pull it up

C

caulking frow–a tool used to jam oakum (a mix of frayed rope, oil, tar, or grease) between the timbers of a ship to keep it sealed watertight

combers–long curving ocean waves powered by high winds

companionway–a hatchway built into a raised windowed structure leading from the ship's deck to the cabins below by way of steep stairs or a ladder

crow's nest–a partially covered platform above the tallest mast (main yard) that serves as a lookout (another term for the *masthead*)

D

dead reckoning–an estimate of a ship's present location based on knowledge of previous position, elapsed time, and estimated speed

deck lighter–also known as *deck prism*, a pointed or pyramid-shaped glass prism hung from the ceiling of a cabin belowdeck, housed in a small opening in the deck above. Hung point-side down, it is designed to reflect light into dark areas belowdecks (a safe alternative to electric, gas, or oil lamps)

ditty box (or *ditty bag*)—a small wooden chest or a canvas bag in which a sailor keeps personal belongings, supplies, and/or tools

dogwatch—a short on-duty period (two hours instead of the usual four) used to allow for meals and to vary the rotation of chores for the crew

duck sailcloth—a type of canvas used for sails, often imported from the Dutch (*doek* is the Dutch word for *cloth*)

F

figurehead—a carved wooden decoration set on the prow (front or bow) of the ship, generally a bust or figure that, in some way, evokes the spirit or history of the vessel

fo'c'sle (abbreviation of *forecastle*)—sailor's quarters and deckhouse in the front of the vessel where supplies may be stored

G

gaff—the pole (spar) that secures the upper edge of a four-cornered sail *gallant*–a flag flying on a smaller mast

galley–kitchen of a ship

H

halyard–the ropes that raise (hoist) a sail attached to a spar (pole)

helm–the ship's wheel

hull–the frame or shell of a ship

L

lanyard–a rope to tie off something

lazaret–a small area of a ship where supplies and provisions are stored

M

mainsail–principal sail on a sailing vessel

mainyard–a horizontal yard (pole) that holds the mainsail

manila rope–a strong flexible type of rope woven from hemp found in the Philippines that does not weaken in salt water

masthead–a small platform set on the mast above the mainyard (horizontal pole) used as a lookout station (another word for the *crow's nest*)

mizzen topsail–the sail just above the lowest sail on the mizzenmast

O

oilskins–outerwear (jackets, pants, hats) made of cloth that has been treated with oil to make it waterproof

out studding sails–hoisting long narrow sails used in addition to the regular sails for use in good weather

P

point–to change the direction of a sailing vessel

poop deck–a raised deck in the rear of the ship that forms the roof over a cabin space below

prow–the front part of a ship that slices through the water–another term for *bow*

R

ratlines–rope ladders that run mast to mast

renipping the buntlines–tightening the ropes fastened to the foot of a sail that have become slack

rigging–the collection of ropes (lines), masts, sails, and yards (poles) that interact with wind in order to sail a ship

rollers–large powerful waves

royal yard–the yard (pole) that holds the royal sail

S

sextant—a navigating tool used to help chart a course or determine the latitude (distance north or south of the equator) of a ship based on the angle of the moon, sun, and stars in relation to the horizon

shrouds—rigging left in place that runs from the masts to the sides of the ship to support the mast

spanker gaff—the pole that supports a special sail called a spanker located at the back (aft) of the ship

spar—a wooden pole that helps secure and support rigging

square-rigger—a ship with sails hung on horizontal yards

stern—back of the ship

strike—to take down a sail

studding sail—long narrow sails used in addition to the regular sails for use in good weather to add sail power

stun'sl—an abbreviation for *studding sail*

T

tack—zigzagging in order to sail into or away from the wind

tarpaulin—a strong waterproof canvas cloth

topgallant spar–the pole that holds the sail above the topsail

topsail–the second sail from the bottom

trestletrees–pair of horizontal beams that support an upper mast

W

watch–a designated amount of time (usually four hours) during which a portion of the crew is on duty

winch–a mechanical device that rotates in order to lift, tighten, or hoist a rope

Y

yard–a pole with tapered ends slung from a mast on which a sail is suspended

yardarm–the outermost end of a yard (pole)

The music to
"The Ballad of Mary Maude Lee"